When I sold my first manuscript, LOVESWEPT was still a dream in the making and I didn't know that a book was measured in words rather than pages. LOVESWEPT and I began together and we grew up together.

It's been a wonderful ten years. I've been privileged to work with some of the best people in the business, and through my books, I've met readers from all over the world, women who truly care about the world and the people in it, women who became instant friends.

Occasionally I'm asked when I'll get around to writing something "serious." That's a little like asking a daffodil when it's going to be a tree. A daffodil is a daffodil and a tree is a tree. And although a tree can provide shelter from the rain, don't try to plant one in the window box.

I'm not really getting off the subject. What I'm trying to do, in my own way, is to explain the sense of pride I take, and have always taken, in being a LOVESWEPT writer.

This is a very special line of romances. They don't cure disease or stop wars but, for a little while, they make us smile. What a wonderful gift to give to the world. And what an honor to be a part of it.

Billie Green

WHAT ARE *LOVESWEPT* ROMANCES?

They are stories of true romance and touching emotion. We believe those two very important ingredients are constants in our highly sensual and very believable stories in the LOVESWEPT *line. Our goal is to give you, the reader, stories of consistently high quality that may sometimes make you laugh, sometimes make you cry, but are always fresh and creative and contain many delightful surprises within their pages.*

Most romance fans read an enormous number of books. Those they truly love, they keep. Others may be traded with friends and soon forgotten. We hope that each LOVESWEPT *romance will be a treasure—a "keeper." We will always try to publish*

LOVE STORIES YOU'LL NEVER FORGET BY AUTHORS YOU'LL ALWAYS REMEMBER

The Editors

Loveswept ® 618

WILDFIRE

BILLIE GREEN

BANTAM BOOKS
NEW YORK · TORONTO · LONDON · SYDNEY · AUCKLAND

WILDFIRE

A Bantam Book / June 1993

If you would be interested in receiving protective vinyl
covers for your Loveswept books, please write to this
address for information:

Loveswept
Bantam Books
P.O. Box 985
Hicksville, NY 11802

ISBN 0-553-44247-3

Published simultaneously in the United States and Canada

Bantam Books are published by Bantam Books, a division of Bantam
Doubleday Dell Publishing Group, Inc. Its trademark, consisting of the
words "Bantam Books" and the portrayal of a rooster, is Registered
in U.S. Patent and Trademark Office and in other countries.
Marca Registrada. Bantam Books, 1540 Broadway, New York,
New York 10036.

PRINTED IN THE UNITED STATES OF AMERICA

OPM   0 9 8 7 6 5 4 3 2 1

To Sally, for the brainstorming session.
You brought the brain,
I provided the storm.

wildfire **1.** any furious, uncontrollable fire **2.** something that acts rapidly and intensely **3.** a sweeping conflagration.

ONE

"Tell her . . . tell her—" Rae Anderson broke off in frustration and blew out a puff of air, stirring a stray lock of auburn hair on her forehead. "Tell her to stop it."

"Gee, why didn't I think of that? That'll probably fix everything."

Hearing the undisguised sarcasm from the woman on the other side of the desk, Rae glanced up. Glenna Baxter, Rae's excellent secretary and even more excellent friend, was a well-padded brunette with a baby doll's face and a field marshal's attitude.

"Well what am I supposed to do?" Rae asked in exasperation. "I've already explained to Miss Rodale that her actions could seriously jeopardize her interests. I've said it on the phone, in a letter, and to her face. What else can I do?"

Glenna raised one precisely plucked eyebrow. "'Her actions could seriously jeopardize her interests'? People don't talk like that, Rae. You have to come right out and tell her that sane people don't go around shooting at meter readers . . . especially not people who are trying to sue the electric company."

With something between a moan and a laugh, Rae covered her face with one hand. "It was only a water pistol."

"The meter reader didn't know that. And since Miss Rodale used a slingshot to launch pieces of candy at him last month, you can understand why the man was a little gun-shy."

"Who would have thought M&M's could raise such ugly little welts?" Rae murmured, pulling at the neck of her cotton blouse. "Is it getting hotter in here? Don't you think we could turn on the air-conditioning . . . just for a little while?"

"Stop whining. Only successful lawyers can afford cool air." The brunette rose to her feet. "Until you get a few more clients, we'll either learn to enjoy perspiration or start shooting at the meter reader ourselves. I'll run next door and get us a cold drink."

As soon as the door closed behind Glenna, Rae leaned back in her chair, her lips curving in a wry smile. More clients, she thought. It sounded like such a simple thing.

Rae knew she was a good lawyer—a damn good lawyer—but in Dicton, Texas, population ten thousand and change, attorneys tended to be passed down from generation to generation.

And then there was that pesky little gender thing. In this part of the country, female lawyers were considered an anomaly. A peculiarity of nature along the lines of a potato shaped like Snoopy. Interesting, but of no earthly use.

But probably the biggest strike against Rae was the fact that she was an outsider, born and raised somewhere other than Dicton. Which meant that the only people willing to give her a chance were either newcomers like herself or those whose cases had been turned down by all the homegrown lawyers, people like crazy old Seraphina Rodale.

Rae liked Dicton. She wanted to make this town her home. And the people here seemed to like her as well. They invited her to their parties and dropped by her office to chat. They brought her home-baked cookies and told her what to do for a cold.

And then they took their business somewhere else.

Picking up a file from her desk, Rae opened it, stared at it for a minute, then closed it, shifting restlessly in her seat.

In the past few months she had found herself falling into weird moods. She had tried telling herself that because she was twenty-eight, something inside was whispering, "It's getting late. It's getting late." She had even told herself that when it came right down to it, she was first and foremost a woman, ordained by Nature to perpetuate the species.

Rae told herself a lot of things, but they were mostly a crock of bull. Her mood had nothing to do with biological clocks or gene pools. It had to do with loneliness, and it had to do with love. Rae wanted a family.

With a little twist of a smile she picked up the photograph from her desk and ran caressing fingers across the face that looked back at her, a smiling young man with strong features and thick, sandy blond hair. And in his eyes, in those tender gray eyes, Rae saw an entire world of sweetness and love.

"You shouldn't have left me, Johnny," she whispered.

If he had had to leave, he should have given her children first. Johnny should have left behind a piece of himself for her to love.

Exhaling a slow, controlled breath, she wished that, at the very least, her late husband had left the way open for another man to father her children. But Johnny had been too wonderful, too perfect. The best lover, the best life partner, the best friend.

No man could measure up to that, and sometimes—not often but sometimes—she resented Johnny for having been so wonderful, for having been so absolutely matchless.

Rae had always known she would marry Johnny. From that first day, the day his family moved next door to hers, Johnny had been her constant companion, a hero in her little-girl eyes, and she had told him then that she would marry him someday.

Later, when it came Johnny's turn to propose, their plans had become more concrete. They would practice law together, and after a few years Johnny would go into politics in order to make the world a better place for their children.

Rae had never doubted that their shared dream for the future would become reality. She hadn't known then that there would be no future for Johnny.

There had been times in the past nine years when Rae's need for a family and one-person-just-for-her had urged her to consider settling for what she could get. And in the time since Johnny's death, there had been men who wanted to marry her, nice men who would have given her a nice life and fathered a couple of nice children.

But Rae couldn't bring herself to accept second best. She wanted—she *needed*—to love someone the way she had loved Johnny.

"Electrifying fizz, energizing sugar, and mysterious chemical compounds for me," Glenna said, as she walked back into the office. "Really boring mineral water for you. No substance, no challenge. I don't see how you can drink this stuff. It tastes like day-old Alka-Seltzer."

As she placed the water-beaded bottle on the desk, the brunette glanced out the window. "Whoa . . . this view is definitely getting better. I swear that man was born knowing how to get a woman's motor started."

Swinging her chair around, Rae looked out the window and felt her heart give a little hop-skip. Standing across the street, smiling down at the mayor's plump wife, was a man with sun-streaked brown hair and an incredibly handsome face. Drew McCallister.

Drew lived on the famed Ashkelon Ranch with his father, John Joseph McCallister. On paper, Drew and his father were partners, but even though the elder McCallister was in his seventies and had been paralyzed from the waist down for almost twenty years, everyone knew that the old man was still in charge. From a wheelchair in the study of Ashkelon, Joe McCallister ruled an empire.

Over the years Joe had acquired money, property, and a reputation for ruthlessness, but because of Drew's nature, the old man hadn't been able to pass his single-minded ambition on to his son. No one in Welch County was more admired or well liked than Drew McCallister. And as Rae stared at him, it occurred to her that for the first time in nine years she was feeling something more than casual interest in a man.

Maybe Drew was responsible for her recent restless moods. Had she finally found a man who could measure up to Johnny?

"Talk about hot." Glenna was still talking, still ogling. "Steam starts to rise every time I look at him. It's not just that he's the sexiest thing alive. It's . . . it's—I don't know. There's always been something a little dangerous about him, as though—"

"You think Drew is dangerous?" Rae broke in, frowning as she studied his features. Even from across the street, the gentleness in Drew's face was evident.

"Drew? Who in hell's talking about Drew?"

Before the words were out of Glenna's mouth, a man stepped from behind an ornamental tree, and Rae knew who her friend was referring to.

Tanner West.

Tanner was not only Ashkelon's foreman, he was Drew's best friend, an association that confounded Rae. She knew that Drew and Tanner had been raised together, and from what she had heard, no one could ask for a better overseer than the latter.

But the men's personal relationship simply didn't make sense. How could someone as kind, decent, and rock-solid as Drew have a man like Tanner West for his best friend?

Rising to her feet, Rae joined Glenna at the window, drawn there against her will. A tall, muscular man, Tanner looked like a Roman gladiator done in bronze. His thick black hair was just a little too long and always looked as though it had been combed by a wild Texas wind. The tight, faded jeans he wore had been aged to a softness that displayed every hard muscle in his buttocks and thighs. And, although she couldn't see it from across the street, she knew that a demon's light glittered in those dark, deep-set eyes.

Rae didn't like him. She didn't like him at all. But every now and again she wondered if her feelings for Tanner were based on the kind of man he was or if she disliked him because he so obviously disliked her.

They had met several weeks after Rae moved to Dicton, on the night of the Lone Dees dance.

Lone Dees, a corruption of a French term for the tenth year, was a local celebration dating back to the early nineteenth century when a group of French Huguenots had decided to make this part of Texas their home. Every ten years the austere farmers would gather together in Dicton to thank

God for bringing them to this new land and to brag about their farms, their livestock, and their children.

Gradually the celebration changed to reflect the times, and now Lone Dees was a weeklong mingling of carnival rides and livestock shows, auctions and beauty pageants, parades and fireworks displays. The dance, held on the crepe-paper-bedecked town square, was the chaotic event that brought the festival to a close.

For Rae, Lone Dees was a perfect introduction to the town. Everyone, old and young, rich and poor, participated, and they were all friendly, all welcoming.

But on the night of the dance, as the shadows began to fall on the long summer day and all around her people were partnered for dances or flirtatious conversation, Rae had felt a pricking loneliness nudge against her. And that was when she spotted the man leaning against the wall at the edge of an unlit alley.

He stood alone in the shadows, tall and dark, his attention held by a group of children who were mimicking their parents with an overly exuberant version of the two-step.

As though he felt her curious gaze on him, the man began to turn toward her. In the next instant the sky over the town square came alive with fireworks, spotlighting the interlude, exaggerating its importance. His rugged features and shadowy eyes, illuminated by erratic bursts of distant light, caught at her imagination and held her still.

Only for the briefest of moments did they stand and stare at each other, but in that moment Rae felt a flash of communication, incredibly intense and unlike anything she had experienced before.

Because in his eyes, eyes dark enough to be mistaken for black, Rae had recognized a deep, restless hunger so powerful and so disturbingly familiar that she had been forced to look away from the sight.

The whole episode had been over in a matter of seconds, and in the following days, she was forced to admit that her imagination had been getting out of hand, in what was locally known as Lone Dees madness. The excitement of the celebration had caught her in its grip and played tricks with her mind.

When Rae had next met Tanner, there was nothing in his eyes except taunting, scornful animosity. Because his attitude was so obvious, Rae had assumed it was a personality trait, that he was antagonistic to everyone, but after seeing him interact with other people in town, she had changed her mind. With everyone else, either he was casually polite or he ignored them completely. His hostility was reserved for Rae.

Now, as she watched him from across the street,

Tanner was once again evoking unwanted reactions in her. Sweet heaven, even the way he moved was an affront to decent folk. Tanner West, with his sensual mouth and desperado eyes, was not a respectable man.

Rae felt her muscles contract in irresistible anger and, as on that night two years ago, the sight of him left her so unsettled that she had to look away.

"I don't know what this town would do without Tanner to gossip about," Glenna said. "He's been raising hell and eyebrows, not to mention expectations, for as long as I've known him. Getting drunk, starting fights . . . I told you about the time he rode that wild horse of his right through the middle of Eddie and Louise Wheeler's backyard barbecue." She cut her eyes toward Rae. "The funny thing is, Drew always defends him."

"Funny? No, that's the kind of man Drew is."

"I guess so." The brunette's voice was doubtful. "To tell you the truth, I've always thought of Drew as a little bit ordinary, but the way he stands up for Tanner is pretty damn high class if you ask me. Even back when that gas-station thing happened, Drew—"

"What gas-station thing?"

"You mean I didn't tell you about that? Tanner must have been about seventeen when it happened. Oh my gosh, was it really eighteen years ago? Rae,

I'm getting old! How could eighteen years have gone by? I'm only five years older than you, but look at you and look at me. Why didn't I get your complexion? Or your figure? I can't even grow decent fingernails. It's not fair. Especially since you—"

"Glenna . . . the gas station?"

"What? Oh, yeah." The brunette stopped patting her throat with the back of her hand and took a swallow of her drink as she leaned against the window. "Well, rumor had it that Tanner was involved in a robbery at Hardy's Texaco. Lordy, the gossip was flying that week. But nothing ever came of it because Old Joe paid Pete Hardy to drop the charges. At least that was the story that went around. Some people say that's why Tanner works so hard for so little pay, because Old Joe's holding that robbery over his head. Which is stupid when you think about it. I mean, the statute of limitations probably ran out years ago." Glenna shrugged. "Who knows? I'm just grateful he stays. He adds a little spice to this town. He always looks like he just got out of bed." She grinned. "Somebody else's bed."

"You were right the first time," Rae said slowly. "Tanner West is a dangerous man."

"Yeah," Glenna said dreamily, sighing as she turned away from the window. "Back to work. I guess I'd better get to the post office." Suddenly her eyes brightened. "Maybe I'll walk today. If Tanner stays put, I just might happen to run into him."

When the other woman grabbed up a handful of envelopes from the desk and rushed out of the room, Rae laughed and returned to her chair.

Nothing that Glenna had told her came as any great shock. She wouldn't put anything past Tanner. But the fact that her friend hadn't expected Drew's defense of Tanner did surprise her. It was exactly the kind of thing Drew would do. Because Drew was the kind of man Johnny would have become, if he had been given the chance. A man whose personal integrity was never in doubt, a man whose sense of loyalty was unquestionable.

She glanced again at the framed portrait on her desk. Johnny would have been thirty-two now. Only a little younger than Drew. And although physically the two men were nothing alike, there was the same look of innate sweetness about them. Drew was calm and assured, like Johnny, and Drew held the same concern for his fellow man.

Drew McCallister would do all the things Johnny had not been given the chance to do. He would be the kind of father who set a solid, loving example for his children. And the woman lucky enough to become his wife would be cherished, truly and deeply cherished. Drew would—

"Dreaming erotic dreams, Rae?"

Even as her eyes flew open, Rae already knew who had invaded the private territory of her thoughts. Tanner's low, husky voice was unmistakable.

The door to the outer office stood open, and he leaned lazily against the frame, watching her with those dark devil's eyes.

After a moment he pushed away from the door and moved on into the room. "Is this what you do all day? Sit in here and think sexy thoughts? Naked bodies, hot and sweaty, all tangled up together? Is that what keeps you going? Do you—"

"Why are you here, Tanner?" she interrupted, her tone indifferent.

His shrug was brief, a casual movement of broad shoulders. "I'm just your average tourist, paying a visit to foreign climes. See, I had a sudden yen to step across the line and stand elbow to elbow with moral probity. You're a native, Rae, so maybe you can tell me . . . Does goodness always feel so damned dusty?"

Raising one brow, she tapped her pen impatiently on the desk, silently urging him to get to the real reason for his visit.

He gazed at her just long enough to make her shift in her chair before saying, "Joe wants you to come out to the ranch this afternoon. A couple of people have dropped dead, so his will needs revising."

The tapping stopped as Rae's hand froze in mid-air. "Me?" she squeaked, her eyes widening in surprise. "Old Joe . . . I mean, Mr. McCallister wants *me* to revise his will? Are you sure that's what he said?"

"Joe isn't an easy man to misunderstand. He mostly talks at the top of his lungs."

After staring at her pen for a second, Rae raised her gaze to Tanner. "But why me? Everyone—at least everyone of Joe McCallister's stature— uses Donnie Lee." Donnie Lee Coker was not only born and raised in Dicton, he had practiced law there for more than thirty years.

"Why me?" she repeated.

Tanner took a seat in the chair across from her, then slid down and slung one leg over the padded arm. Only when he was comfortable did he turn his attention to her question.

"It probably has to do with the fact that Joe and Coker were some kind of rivals back in their wild and woolly days. For the past twenty or thirty years, Joe has been using Amos Roach over in Kliester, but since Amos is one of the ones who dropped dead, he decided to give you a shot. He wants you to start with the will and see how that goes, then maybe he'll turn over the rest of it to you."

"That doesn't explain why he asked for *me*. There are plenty of other lawyers in town for him to choose from. Jake Watkins . . . Obie Jennings . . . Doesn't T. J. Goolsby specialize in agricultural law?"

"Now I see why you don't have any clients," Tanner said wryly. "I'm sure there are a lot of reasons why he picked you, but the main one is, using you will put Coker's big fat nose out of joint."

His grin was slightly malicious. "You have to admire Joe. It's a neat, unmistakable insult. By tomorrow morning everyone in Welch County will know Joe would rather use an outsider, a female to boot, than go to Donnie Lee Coker."

Now that sounded like something Joe McCallister would do, Rae conceded silently. Back in his heyday, the elder McCallister's feuds had been as famous as his extramarital affairs.

"John Joseph McCallister wants *me* to revise his will," she murmured aloud, shaking her head in amazement.

Tanner chuckled. "Now you're getting it. And here's a bonus for you: If you take your time with all the legal mumbo jumbo, draw out the whereases and heretofores, you might even get to stay for dinner. Does the thought of sitting at the same table with Drew make you hot, Rae?"

At the change in Tanner's tone she glanced up

sharply. He had moved and was now leaning across her desk. Before she could stop him, he reached out and began to twine a single auburn curl around his forefinger.

Rae flinched, jerking her head away. And then uneasiness gave way to anger. *He had no right*. He had no right to stand there casually touching her hair. Casually touching her private thoughts and feelings.

As he kept his gaze trained on her face, Tanner's dark eyes narrowed, and he let out a long, low whistle.

"Voodoo woman," he said, his normally husky voice growing deeper. "When you get mad, you don't look like somebody's kid sister anymore. Those baby-blue eyes look like opals . . . like lightning in the tropics. You ought to get mad around Drew sometime, Rae. Then he might actually see you."

Swearing a silent curse, Rae exhaled a short, exasperated breath. She knew better than to let him see her anger. Any reaction at all from her would only add to his enjoyment.

Gritting her teeth, she watched in silence as Tanner moved around to her side of the desk and leaned against it, his long legs inches away from hers.

"You know what your problem is?" he asked, still watching her.

She tilted her chair back, raising her head to meet his dark gaze. "Yes," she said flatly, "men who are dense enough to think I'm interested in their opinions."

He chuckled softly. "No, your problem is you. You've got the wrong idea about yourself. Somewhere along the line—it probably started back when you were still in the cradle—somebody told you that you were a good little girl, and like an idiot, you bought it. Which is why you've spent your whole life living a lie, wondering why you don't feel easy in your own skin."

"You know nothing about me," she said tightly.

"Maybe, maybe not. Sometimes I get this crazy idea about you. Sometimes I think maybe there's fire in you. And not a tame little Girl Scout fire either. Wildfire, Rae. Burning hot and hard . . . like on the night I first saw you."

He paused just long enough for the memory of a starburst-charged moment to fill the space between them.

"Lone Dees madness," he murmured. "It was all right there in your eyes for anyone to see. Do you know how many babies are born nine months after Lone Dees? Is that what it was, Rae? Do we have to wait another ten years for what's inside you to come spilling out? Or is it always there, waiting for the rest of the world to catch up?"

He smiled. "One thing's certain, if it's there, you don't know what to do with it. That's why you keep it hidden and pretend like it doesn't exist. But I'll tell you something, sweetness"—although he hadn't moved, when his voice dropped to a husky whisper, he seemed closer—"if it's there, and if you ever decided to let it out in the open, you'd have men howling after you like freakin' alley cats, tearing at each other's throats just to get a chance at being the one chosen to service you."

Rae's breath caught in a soft gasp, and she closed her eyes to block out the sight of him. "Do you have to be so crude?" she asked, her voice stiff and hoarse.

"What's your problem? 'Service' is a perfectly respectable word. I could have said they would all want to f—"

"Stop it!"

Rae was furious, not a new sensation in her dealings with Tanner, but this time she was more angry with herself than with him. Why in hell did she fall into every single trap he set for her?

"Relax." There was a definite hint of laughter in his voice now. "I said sometimes I think that. The idea is too incredible to last very long. Because you really are a good little girl. Aren't you?"

Forcing the stiffness from her spine, Rae opened

her eyes and shot an irritated glance in his direction. "Don't you have something to do? Somewhere to go?"

Instead of answering, he reached behind him to pick up the framed picture from her desk. "So this is the fabled Saint Johnny," he said slowly. "The late husband for whom you still pine." He cut his eyes toward her. "He looks more like your brother than your husband. He has that same wholesome, All-American, good-as-gold look."

Slowly, carefully, she took the portrait from Tanner's hands and placed it on the far corner of her desk, out of his reach.

"How do you know about Johnny?"

He reacted with a short, harsh laugh. "That's a stupid question. You've been in this town long enough to know how it works."

Yes, Rae knew how it worked. She had come to Dicton because she found big-city law in a big-city firm too impersonal. She had dreamed of a small practice that would allow her to give each client the personal attention he or she deserved. But one of the drawbacks of small-town life was that everyone's business was everyone's business.

Less than a month after she had moved here from Fort Worth, Rae had run into a chatty stranger in the drugstore and had been staggered to learn that the woman not only knew what kind of shampoo Rae used, she also knew that Rae wrote to her parents every Monday without fail.

"I know things about you that you wouldn't believe," Tanner was saying now. "You want me to tell you what you wear to bed? A pink, candy-striped cotton nightshirt. Wholesome gear. Virtuous. But I also know that sometimes in the middle of the night, the little candy-striped nightshirt starts to feel restrictive. So you strip it off . . . and for the rest of the night there's nothing but air and freedom between your body and the sheets."

Rae felt furious heat flood her face. This time she counted to ten before she spoke.

"I've heard a lot of rumors about you," she said slowly, "but no one mentioned the fact that you were a Peeping Tom along with all the rest."

"Didn't they?" He raised one dark brow. "Now that surprises me. I didn't think there was any sin, any deviant behavior, that hadn't been laid on me. As it happens, I haven't been peeking through the windows of your chaste little bedroom. Not that I wouldn't like to. Oh yes, I'll have to give that idea some thought . . . because since the first time I set eyes on you, I've been wondering about that red hair of yours."

He paused, letting his gaze travel slowly down her body. "I've been wondering if the color runs true. You know, I can close my eyes right now and see how that peculiar shade of red would look against the smooth, creamy skin of your belly."

Rae had to grip the arms of her chair to keep from flying at him. Tanner had gone too far this time. He was standing in her office—a place of business, for pity's sake—in broad daylight, and he was calmly talking about pubic hair. *Her* pubic hair!

She wanted to tell him he had no right to imagine her naked, that he had no right to make her feel so exposed, so vulnerable. But she didn't say any of that. She didn't so much as blink an eye.

"You mean there's actually something about me that you don't know?" she asked, leaning forward to pick up her pen. "What happened to the famous small-town grapevine?"

This time his husky laugh held genuine amusement. "Just give me time. You never know, maybe I'll drop by Rusty's Tavern some Thursday night. I think Dr. Vaughn is usually there on Thursdays."

Mention of the local gynecologist brought Rae's head up sharply. He wouldn't. He couldn't—

And then she saw the look in his eyes and knew he had suckered her again.

"Will you please—" she began.

"Or maybe I'll just leave it to my imagination," he murmured, as though he were actually giving the matter serious thought. "We could make that the ultima Thule of our relationship. They say a little mystery keeps a friendship alive, and to tell you the truth, ours could use some help, because I know so damned much about you and your worthy little life."

"Tanner, would you please—"

"You were nineteen when you married the boy next door. Our hero, Johnny." He nodded toward the picture. "He was twenty-three, a brilliant student, an athlete with a room full of trophies, already in law school when you married him. He was being groomed for a career in politics like his father. The next Bobby Kennedy, they said."

He paused, rubbing his chin with a thumb, as though weighing his next words. "But then when you'd been married for seven months, your Johnny got careless. He dove into a lake, hit an underwater rock, and broke his neck."

The words, spoken without inflection, brought back a flash flood of memories—terror and pain, guilt and rage, and the ever-present unquenchable loneliness.

"And I know that his were the last human hands to touch you." Relentlessly Tanner went on, his deep-set eyes measuring her reactions as he spoke. "But since Johnny Anderson was a saint, you might say he doesn't count. You probably still qualify as a virgin. And I'd take a guess that he was one of the fools who perpetuated that trash about your being a good little girl."

"Johnny wasn't a fool," Rae ground out. "Don't talk about him. Don't ever—" She broke off abruptly and clamped her teeth together as she struggled for composure.

"Say it," Tanner urged in a low whisper.

He was leaning close now, so close, she could feel his breath on her face and see that his eyes were ablaze with the wild, demonic light.

"Let go, Rae," he said, his voice low and hoarse. "For once in your life, really cut loose. Let it all come pouring out, so hard and fast that it takes me under. Come on, tell me I'm not fit to breathe Johnny's name. Tell me I'm an arrogant devil who'll burn in hell for blaspheming your deity."

She drew in several short, shaky breaths. "Johnny wasn't a god," she said finally, the words unsteady. "And he wasn't a saint. He was simply the best man I've ever known."

Two beats later he straightened away from her with a short, contemptuous laugh. "Poor Drew. If you ever catch him, he'll always be second best. He'll never quite measure up to the ghost of love past."

"Drew doesn't have to compete with anyone," she said tightly. "He wouldn't even try. He has too much integrity, too much sensitivity, to attack a dead man."

He studied her face for a long moment. "You think you know Drew, don't you?"

As he spoke, Rae thought she caught a flash of that strange, restless hunger, but it was gone too quickly for her to be sure.

Seconds later when he pushed away from her desk, there was no emotion at all in his eyes. "I guess I'll leave you to your dusty little dreams now."

He sounded bored, as though he had suddenly grown tired of baiting her. With a perfunctory "See you around," he turned and began to move toward the door.

"Tanner?"

When he paused to glance over his shoulder, Rae raised her gaze from her still-trembling fingers and met his eyes. "You've had a fun half hour, getting on my nerves, saying stupid things, but—" She moistened her lips. "You don't go around saying these things about me to . . . to anyone else, do you?"

"You mean, does Drew know that your almost-but-not-quite virginal heart beats faster for him? I don't know. Probably not. Modest is our Drew. He doesn't know he's the most eligible bachelor in the county." He raised one dark brow. "Anything else?"

"As a matter of fact there is." She relaxed her fingers and picked up her pen again. "How did you know about the nightshirt?"

He grinned. "Paula told me."

"Paula? I don't know anyone named Paula."

"She's a salesgirl at Beatty's. You were shopping there the other day, and when she tried to sell you a cotton candy-striped nightshirt, you very politely explained why it just wouldn't do for you."

A sound of exasperation escaped her. "And now it's all over town? That's ridiculous."

He smiled. "Not all over town. In fact I imagine Paula forgot all about it by the next day. But I just happened to see her that night. And I just happened to bring up the subject of Dicton's good little lady lawyer."

Pausing at the door, he turned to look her over one last time. The demonic light had been extinguished, and now there was nothing more than superficial interest in his eyes.

"You won't get Drew, you know. That's a shame, really. You might be a good match for him, and having you out at Ashkelon would definitely make the place more interesting. But the fact is, sweetness, you haven't got a prayer. If you stay for dinner tonight, you'll see why."

And then he walked out, leaving Rae torn between curiosity and exasperation.

TWO

The white rock road threw up clouds of dust behind the Volvo as Rae drove west toward Ashkelon.

Today she was putting her professional life on the line. It was that simple. If Old Joe liked her, she had it made, because others in town would automatically follow his lead. But—and this was probably the most important but in Rae's career— if the elder McCallister decided he didn't like her, she might as well pack up her law books, take out her knitting, and start living on the money Johnny had left her. Because although Joe McCallister wouldn't tell people not to use Rae, word would quickly get around that he had found her unsatisfactory, and then not even eccentrics like Seraphina Rodale would bring her their business.

Drawing in a bracing breath, she loosened her

grip on the steering wheel. It was too late to worry about it now. And as Johnny used to say, the sweetest apples were always out at the end of the shakiest limbs.

For the past couple of miles Rae had been driving alongside the white board fence that marked McCallister property. Now she spotted the gate with a tall white arch over it. A single word, ASHKELON, was painted in neat black lettering on the crosspiece of the arch. There was nothing ostentatious about the McCallister standard. It was simple and clean. Aristocratic.

Slowing almost to a stop, she turned onto the paved milelong drive that led to the ranch house. The drive was also bordered by white board fence, tied into occasional barbed-wire cross sections.

A quarter of a mile up the drive, she passed a wooden side gate that gave access to the gravel road leading to the ranch's outbuildings. In the near distance she could see a handful of men working together to put up a new section of corral fence.

As Rae drew nearer, one of the men straightened and moved away from the others.

Tanner.

He was shirtless, his tanned, muscular flesh glistening with perspiration in the bright June sun, tight jeans following the outline of his lean hips.

It was incredible. Even from this distance Rae

felt that Tanner was seeing things he couldn't possibly see, looking through the metal of the car, through flesh and bones, right to the center of her.

Catching her gaze on him, he brought his index finger to his forehead in a mocking salute, laughing when she acknowledged him with a short nod.

As she drove past, she had to fight the urge to look in her rearview mirror to see if his attention was still turned toward her. She cursed him silently for being Tanner, for disrupting her thoughts on this important day.

Moments later, when a two-story white house with green shutters and precise landscaping came into sight, Rae shoved Tanner West out of her mind. She didn't have time to worry about him today.

"Don't go to the front door," Glenna had warned. "Even the governor uses the side door at Ashkelon."

Parking in the small, paved lot at the side of the house, Rae stepped from the Volvo and reached in for her briefcase. After taking a moment to smooth one hand over the skirt of her navy-blue suit, she started up the walk.

On the other side of the tall hedge bordering the walk was the pool. Rae couldn't see it, but she knew it was there. Glenna had told her.

In the past the McCallisters had been gregarious folk, every weekend an occasion for a party. Movie stars and world leaders had been entertained in this house. Since Joe's stroke, there weren't so many parties, but Rae could tell that the house remembered. The memory of its encounters with fame was evident in every immaculate line.

Before Rae reached the side door, it was opened by a stout woman in her early fifties. Feena Tease, the McCallisters' housekeeper, attended the same church as Rae, and they had spoken on several occasions, but now a brisk nod was the only indication the older woman gave that they had ever met.

"Mr. McCallister is in his study," Mrs. Tease said, turning to lead the way.

As she followed the housekeeper through a vast family room, Rae caught a glimpse of the pool through a long row of windows. Next they traveled down a hall, making a couple of turns before her guide stopped outside an open door.

"She's here," the other woman called out loudly, and before Rae had time to blink, Mrs. Tease was gone.

Drawing in a steadying breath, Rae moved through the doorway, then stopped abruptly. She had been told of the elder McCallister's collection of first-edition books, but nothing she had heard had prepared her for what she saw now. Every wall was lined with bookshelves. From floor to ceiling, in every direction, there were books. The number was staggering, overwhelming to the uninitiated, which Rae most definitely was.

It took a moment for her to realize that the room contained other things. An antique horsehair settee and heavy wine-colored drapery. A scattering of plants and an impressive collection of Oriental porcelain.

And last but by no means least, in a wheelchair behind a massive mahogany desk, shouting into a telephone, was the man Rae had come to see.

John Joseph McCallister must have once been a powerful man. His upper body still looked strong, his posture erect, his shoulders broad. Although his hair was snow white—in startling contrast to coal-black eyebrows—there was nothing feeble about Joe McCallister. Even if his voice hadn't filled the room, his presence would have.

"Do you think I give a flying fig for your stupid management screwups? I need that equipment, and by God, I need it yesterday! Now get off your bony ass and *ship me my damn bailers!*"

He slammed down the receiver and without pausing to draw breath said, "Here's the deal. My cousin's wife passed away, and I don't feel any need to provide for her squirrelly daughters. I'm richer than I was when I made the will, so I can do more for some of my long-term personnel, but I'm also meaner, so there are a couple of people I want to cut out."

He pulled a manila envelope from a drawer and tossed it across the desk to her. "There it is. Sit down and I'll tell you exactly what I want done."

Short and sweet. This was a man who knew what he wanted and wasn't going to put up with people who wasted his time. Rae could deal with that.

She sat down and went to work.

Little more than an hour later they were wrapping it up. Rae glanced up from her copy of the will. "And you say you want to leave the codicil as it is?"

He turned his head toward her, his gaze growing sharper. "Why? What's wrong with it?"

"The language grows a little ambiguous here." She paused. "It's not very likely, but it could possibly cause Drew trouble later, after you're gone."

"I don't want to hear 'not very likely' and 'possibly.' If the damn thing's wrong, fix it. What in hell do you think you're here for?"

Flipping through the pages of his copy, Joe located the section in question and studied it for several minutes.

"Why didn't I notice that? Why the hell didn't Amos notice it?" He shot a look of grudging admiration her way. "When Tanner told me you were sharp, I thought he was either crazy or working some deal of his own, but I'll be damned if he didn't know what he was talking about."

Rae's brow creased in confusion. Tanner told him she was sharp? Tanner despised her. Why on earth would he help her out by recommending her to Joe McCallister?

Glancing up, she saw that the old man was now leaning back in his chair, staring at the ceiling.

"I want to make sure everything is in order," he murmured, "just in case I kick off anytime soon. There's a damned epidemic of it. People dropping like flies."

He lowered his gaze from the ceiling and caught her watching him. "The boys have worked hard, damned hard, to make this place what it is. I want them taken care of." He moved his head restlessly. "Tanner won't get much. He doesn't expect anything, but he's earned his share. I have to give him that. No matter what he does in his free time, he never misses a day's work. And when he first started, back when he was just a kid, it was backbreaking labor. I had the crazy idea I could work that bad streak out of him." He shook his head. "It didn't happen. He would do every job I set out for him without complaining, do it better than men twice his age, then he'd go out and raise hell just the same as always."

Feeling that some comment was expected of her, Rae said, "He certainly seems different from Drew."

The old man reacted with a gruff bark of laughter. "Night and day. I always said that. Different as night and day. Look in Drew's eyes, and you'll see peace. Look in Tanner's, and you'll see the fires of hell raging. I don't think the boy will ever be at peace."

Then, as though talking about Tanner somehow disturbed him, Joe fell into a brooding silence.

Shifting restlessly in her chair, Rae cleared her throat and said, "Glenna tells me Drew graduated from A&M at the top of his class."

"Glenna? Glenna Baxter?" The old man was suddenly alert again. "She had a smart-ass attitude as a girl, and I can't see how turning into a woman has changed her much. Not that she's not right about Drew. A man couldn't ask for a better son. Even though his mother spoiled him some, I made sure she didn't ruin him. I might have had to drag Tanner out of trouble a few times, but not Drew. No, it was always Tanner. From the very first, he was either working with the men, in here reading my books, or out beating the crap out of somebody. How do you figure somebody like that? The pieces just don't fit."

He let out a slow breath. "He never picked on anyone smaller or weaker, I'll say that for him. In fact, he usually fought men three times his size. But he could never tell me what the fights were about. Oh, he'd say something like the guy was a butt-head and needed hitting, but he couldn't tell me the real reason. Sometimes I think that when Tanner fights, he isn't attacking a person at all. I think he's trying to work out something inside himself, something that even he doesn't understand."

Joe stopped talking and rubbed his face with a hand that trembled slightly. It was the first sign of age Rae had seen in him.

A moment later, however, he managed to shake off whatever was troubling him and gave a short laugh. "I've been rambling, but I'm not going to apologize. Even if I weren't paying for your time, one of the pleasures of being old and rich is that I can say whatever I damn well please and people have to put up with it."

He pushed the wheelchair away from the desk. "It's time for my nap. You've got two days to work out those changes."

And with the quiet whir of an electric motor, John Joseph McCallister was gone.

Rae sat with her head turned toward the door for a moment before slipping her copy of the will into her briefcase and rising to her feet. Only as she moved toward the door did it hit her.

She had won.

Even though Joe hadn't said a word about her handling the rest of his legal affairs, today was a victory. Because working for Joe McCallister, even in a minor way, would be a signal to the town. What two years of hard work hadn't done, an hour with one old man had. Rae was in.

When she stepped out of the study, she paused, uncertain which way to go. She had been too nervous to pay attention when she had followed Mrs. Tease. Had they approached from the right or from the left?

"Maybe I should wet my finger and check for wind direction," she muttered, feeling slightly foolish. And she would feel even more foolish if she had to stand around in the hall until someone came along to rescue her.

She should have unraveled a ball of twine on her way in, she decided, and a smile twitched at her lips at the thought of casting John Joseph McCallister as the Minotaur. She had definitely felt a little sacrificial during the first few minutes of their time together.

"Meditating again, Rae?"

The husky voice sent her whirling around. Tanner stood a few feet down the hall, leaning against the wall as he inspected her neatly dressed figure.

"I should have known," she muttered under her breath. "Hello, Tanner."

Although he had put on a shirt, and had even managed to fasten a couple of the buttons, Tanner still looked out of place. Stained Stetson, scuffed and dusty boots, blue chambray work shirt with a corner tear in the sleeve. Tanner was Ashkelon's manager, but he looked more like a vagrant, hired for a couple days' work.

There had been a spark of something, some unidentifiable emotion, in his dark eyes when she first turned to him, but now, as she continued to study him, the spark faded, and his lips twisted in a contemptuous smile.

"So how do you like the old wickiup?" he asked, waving a hand at the surroundings. "Are you going to get to see more of it? Staying for dinner, Rae?"

"Apparently I'm more efficient than you thought. I finished too soon and wasn't invited."

Having done the polite-conversation bit, she started to walk away, but she stopped when she heard his lazy voice. "You're going the wrong way."

She counted to ten and turned to walk in the opposite direction. After taking a couple of steps, she stopped again and glanced back. "Why did you recommend me to Mr. McCallister?"

"Don't you know? I did it to annoy you."

"That is the most stupid—Why on earth would it annoy me?"

Tanner's lips stretched in a slow smile as he

moved closer. "I learned more than how to run a ranch from Joe. He also taught me some wicked chess moves. You owe me now, Rae. Don't you see the irony? You can't stand the sight of me, but now you're in my debt."

Throwing up a hand, she said, "You have got to be the most incredibly irritating—"

"Did you get a look at Drew's guest on your way in?" he asked abruptly.

Blinking at the sudden change of subject, she studied his face. And then she understood. This was what Tanner had been referring to earlier, the thing that was supposed to show Rae why she didn't stand a chance with Drew.

Refusing to be drawn into another of his games, she said, "Good-bye, Tanner," and walked away.

He gave a soft laugh. "Run, run, little mouse."

An instant later he caught up with her, grasped her arm, and forcibly changed her direction.

"What—Will you *let go*!" she said in a tight whisper, glancing around nervously.

"Gonna hit me, sweetness?" he asked, laughing. "Go ahead, I'd like it."

As he pulled her after him, down the hall and up the narrow back stairs, Rae had to either go along with him or go limp and sit on the floor. And she was pretty sure her already bruised dignity wouldn't survive the latter.

On the second floor he walked her into a small sitting room and finally stopped before a window. "I wanted you to see the view from up here," he said calmly.

As an explanation for his actions, it fell short, but rather than argue the point, Rae looked out the window.

Directly below them was the swimming pool. On the surrounding patio were clusters of potted greenery and tables capped with yellow-striped umbrellas. Bright sunlight hit the water, making the pool look like a bowl full of blue diamonds. Resting on one of the tables was a tray of drinks.

It was all very pretty, very pleasant, and although Rae didn't know what she was supposed to be looking at, the pool had given her some idea of where she was. She would be able to find her way out now.

But then, at the instant she made the decision to leave, at the very moment she began to turn away, Rae saw what Tanner had brought her here to see.

Drew was in the pool. And he wasn't alone.

Leaning closer to the window, Rae watched as a woman with long blond hair rose from the water. Her skin was colored gold from the sun, and she wore—

Sweet Pete, Rae thought, nearly choking. Were thong bikinis legal in Welch County?

Here was the definition of voluptuous. And it had little to do with the fact that most of the woman's body was exposed. It was an attitude, her expression, the way she held herself when she walked.

Exhaling a slow breath, Rae shot a look at the man beside her. "Okay, you've had your fun," she said. "She's beautiful and sophisticated, and I'm neither."

She paused and glanced down at her hands, fiddling unnecessarily with the latch on her briefcase. "I've never seen her before . . . but, well, if Drew likes her, I'm sure she's a very nice person."

A short, husky shout of laughter brought her head up. "Nice?" Tanner said, incredulous. "Nice? What a dull little word, definitely not to be used in conjunction with the woman down there. But even if she were *nice*, you can bet that's not what Drew sees in her. And it's not her looks or upper-crust exclusivity. When Drew looks at Lynda, he sees hot, Rae. Capital H-O-T, hot."

With a small troubled frown, Rae shook her head. "No . . . no, you're wrong. Drew isn't like that."

"For Pete's sake, go out and buy a clue." His voice had grown suddenly harsh. "All men are 'like that.' Ants and elephants. Bunny rabbits and Gila monsters. If it's male, it notices hot."

Reluctantly she turned her attention back to the scene below. Hot? What kind of description was that? Then, as Rae watched, the blonde gave Drew a look—just one little look—and an instant later he was out of the pool and at her side.

How did she do it?

Hot, Rae told herself in a grudging, gloomy admission. Lynda was hot.

"Lynda knows how to get a man's attention." At some point, while Rae was caught up in her moody musings, Tanner had moved closer, and now his words were a husky whisper against her ear. "She's had a lot of practice. Not like you, my wholesome friend. Look down there, Rae. Take a real good look. That's the kind of woman Drew brings home and takes on his little trips to Las Vegas. Does she look wholesome to you?"

When she tried to move away from him, he held her in place with an arm at her waist, making her catch her breath in a silent gasp. The heat from his palm seemed to burn right through her suit all the way to her flesh. How could a human hand generate such heat?

The fire in his touch and the stroke of his breath on her ear made it difficult to concentrate. And perhaps that was why Tanner's next words seemed to come, not from him, but from somewhere inside her own head.

"Drew is a good man. So good, he needs a contrast. In Lynda he senses something that's just a little bit dangerous, just a little wild, and he's drawn to that. You see, sweetness, Drew hasn't learned one of the basic facts of life yet. He doesn't know that cereal boxes sometimes mislead you about the prize inside."

Needing desperately to get away from him, from the callused hand and husky voice, Rae turned and pressed her back against the wall, putting a scant few inches between them.

"You've made your point," she said, struggling to keep her voice calm. "I don't know why you went to so much trouble, but I get the idea."

He moved his shoulders in a careless shrug. "Friends are supposed to help each other out. We're friends . . . aren't we, Rae? Somebody had to tell you that you're wasting your dusty little daydreams. You could change your hair, your clothes, and even that blessedly blunt way you talk, but you still wouldn't be hot. Because hot's not on the surface. It's how you handle what's inside you."

His words held her still, the tone and tenor mesmerizing her. After an endless moment she pulled up what strength he hadn't absorbed through his palm and slid sideways, away from him, straightening her jacket in agitation as she moved.

"I don't need you to tell me I could never be like

her," she said without looking at him. "I recognize my own limitations."

"Do you? I doubt it. You could be hot . . . hot enough to start a forest fire. All you need is a couple of lessons." He gave a soft laugh. "Want me to teach you, Rae?"

Ignoring him, which she had been trying to do for two years, Rae swung around to leave. But once again, almost against her will, she found herself turning back to him, examining his features with reluctant curiosity.

"Why do you do this?" she asked. "Why are you always trying to get a rise out of me?"

He leaned against the wall and crossed one long leg over the other. "Who knows? Maybe I'm just the kinda guy who, if the buttons are there, I'm gonna push 'em."

Pulling her gaze slowly from the amusement in his dark desperado eyes, Rae walked away quickly. And this time she didn't stop.

But she should have known that Tanner wasn't through with her yet. She hadn't reached the top of the stairs before she heard his voice again.

"Or maybe I'm attracted to my opposite the same as Drew. Maybe for a town outlaw, a good little lady lawyer is the most intriguing thing around."

THREE

"The mariachi band is nice."

The words were barely out of Glenna's mouth before the waiters—who seemed to have been hand-picked for peevishness—all stopped what they were doing, yelled, "Olé!" then went back to being surly.

It was Friday night, and Rae and Glenna were trying out a new restaurant, Tres Hermanas, along with most of the rest of Dicton. In an area where watching county workers fill potholes was considered high entertainment, the opening of a new restaurant was like having the circus come to town.

When their waiter brought iced tea and an appetizer plate to the table, he knocked over the salt, splashed tea on the table, then glared at the women, his expression daring them to mention his ineptitude.

Watching him leave, Glenna repeated, "The mariachi band is nice."

"The owner should have done a little research," Rae said, shaking her head. "Dicton is too small to support another Mexican restaurant. Reg Neeland has one for upper-income people, and LaDonna Pugh—"

"—has one for the rest of us," Glenna finished for her. "The owner's from Dallas. And everybody knows that nobody knows beans in Dallas. Not even refried ones."

As she spoke, Glenna picked up something small and round and cheesy from the appetizer tray and took a bite. Instantly her eyes widened in surprise. She dropped the unidentified morsel, swallowed half her tea in one gulp, then sat staring at the tray in wary fascination.

After a moment she glanced up. "The mariachi band is nice."

Since the rest of their meal was no better than the appetizers, the restaurant's fate seemed to be sealed. Barely adequate food, grudging service, and an out-of-town owner. Three strikes, you're out. Reg and LaDonna didn't have to worry about competition.

It was as Rae sat drinking coffee and Glenna ate her dessert—something gooey that smelled of cinnamon—that the latter glanced up and, with fork poised midair, stared beyond Rae toward the door.

"Who is *she*?"

Glancing around, Rae saw four people enter the restaurant. Drew, Tanner, and two women. She didn't have to ask who Glenna was talking about. The blonde at the front of the group looked as though she had stepped from the pages of a fashion magazine.

"Lynda," Rae said. "I don't know her last name."

"That woman doesn't need a last name." The brunette shot a glance at Rae. "Is she with Tanner? Please don't tell me she's with Tanner."

Rae shook her head. "Not Tanner. Drew. She's staying out at Ashkelon. I got a glimpse of her last week when I went out to talk to Old Joe."

"Look at the way she moves. No, wait, they're passing right behind you. Don't look yet," Glenna added quickly. "Look at that hair. What do rich women do to their hair to make it look so . . . so *rich*? Look at the way she—"

"Will you stop telling me to look? Didn't your mother ever tell you that staring is rude?"

Glenna exhaled what was a cross between a groan and a sigh. "You don't see people like that in Dicton. She's sophisticated. She's pampered. She's—"

"Hot," Rae said, her voice clipped.

"Yeah, that's it. That's it exactly. She's hot."

Crumpling her napkin, Rae dropped it on the table. "Are you through with that goo yet? I'm ready to go."

"Let me make a quick trip to the ladies' room first. I want to pass by their table and get a better look. I hate her, Rae. I really actually totally hate her. She's at the same table with Tanner, and she makes every other woman in town look like Broomhilda in comparison. Why doesn't she go back to where she came from and leave our men . . ."

Glenna was still muttering as she walked away. Rae, alone now at the table, stared steadily at the outsized sombrero on the opposite wall, using it as a focus to keep her eyes from drifting in the direction of Drew's table. She didn't want to see Lynda with her rich-looking hair and her Hot factor. She didn't want to be reminded that—

"You're looking especially wholesome tonight."

With an inward groan Rae raised her chin and turned her head toward the voice. Tanner stood beside the table. Tonight he wore a white western-cut shirt with his jeans. His boots were polished, his hair almost neat.

It was the first time she had seen him since that day at Ashkelon. But unfortunately out of sight, out of mind didn't work when Tanner was involved.

By recommending her to Old Joe, he had made it impossible for her to ignore his existence.

After Rae had finished work on Joe McCallister's will, the old man hadn't given her a single sign of approval, but neither had he criticized. And according to Glenna, when you were dealing with John Joseph McCallister, the absence of criticism was the equivalent of high praise. As a result, although none of the cases were big or spectacular, her practice was definitely picking up.

In fact, Rae would have been feeling a little smug about her future in Dicton except for one thing. Every time a new client walked into her office, she was forced to remember that Tanner was responsible, which was exactly the result he had been hoping for.

"Hello, Tanner," she said, keeping her voice even.

With a short laugh he swung a chair around from the next table and straddled it, folding his forearms on the back as he ran his gaze over her stiff features.

"Hello, Rae." His tone mocked her politeness; his dark eyes gleamed with reckless mischief. "I just thought I'd stop by to see how you're feeling. Lukewarm? Room temperature?" When she shot him a look, he laughed again. "Definitely frost-bitten."

"Has it ever occurred to you that I am just exactly how I want to be?"

"Nope." The word was amused but uncompromising.

"You are what you are because other people told you this is what you should be. You were never given a choice. You can't tell me that when you were a little girl in pigtails somebody gave you a list and you checked off 'Repressed.' Uh-uh. I don't buy it."

Her lips tightened. "I am not repressed. I just don't happen to be obvious."

He moved his shoulders in a brief shrug. "Sometimes obvious is what it takes. If you think Drew is going to start carrying a shovel so he can dig down to the real you, think again. It's like the old joke about talking to a mule. First you have to hit it in the head with a two-by-four to get its attention."

He rubbed his chin with the knuckle of his index finger, studying her with those unnerving dark eyes. "Why don't you switch your sights to someone who can appreciate your less than obvious charms? Bud Arnold over at the post office is looking for a woman, has been for twenty years now. His requirements aren't what you would call exacting. If you can cook, you're in. Or maybe you'd prefer someone who still has hair. Let's see . . . Jerry Don Boyd just got a divorce. His wife took him to the cleaner's, so right now all Jerry Don needs is a good listener."

When she stubbornly refused to comment, he rose to his feet and swung the chair back around. "And then of course there's me," he said, his husky voice taunting her. "I've always loved a challenge."

He watched her, taking in the way the fingers of her right hand clenched around the paper napkin, and then, with a low, lingering laugh, he turned and walked away.

An hour later, when Rae walked into her small house, she was still fuming. Throwing her purse on the couch, she walked straight through to her bedroom and stood in front of the full-length mirror. First she examined her face close up, then she stepped back and studied herself from a distance, turning first this way, then that.

Her auburn hair was pulled back in a French twist, but as usual a few curls had escaped on her forehead and at her temples. Her dress, pale blue linen trimmed with white piping, was attractive and well made. Her figure wasn't bad. There were the required number of curves with no unsightly bulges. Her skin was her best feature. Smooth and creamy. Not a blemish, not a single freckle.

She looked nice and friendly. An objective person might even be moved to say she was pretty. In a wholesome, good-as-gold sort of way.

Swinging away from her reflection, she flopped back on her bed. Damn his eyes, Tanner was right. She looked like somebody's kid sister.

The next day Rae entered her okay-so-I'm-dull phase. For a week she wore her dowdiest clothes and no makeup other than powder. Once, she even showed up for work with her hair pulled back in a tight little bun, causing Glenna to choke on her breakfast Twinkie.

But then on the following Friday, as she sat trying to wade through a year of Seraphina Rodale's electricity bills, something happened to Rae. Something unfolded inside her, a little piece of personal growth that took her by surprise.

She had paused in her work, resting her chin on the palm of one hand to gaze at Johnny's picture, when out of the blue, it occurred to her that she had never fought for anything in her life.

Her parents were wealthy and kind; she was an only child, healthy, intelligent, and relatively conformable; she had fallen in love with Johnny as a child, and he loved her back; she had been hired by a well-established law firm while still at law school.

It was a pattern. All of it, everything Rae had ever wanted, had been handed to her. Not once had she been forced to pursue, to struggle to achieve. She had never had to use her determination and ingenuity to get what she wanted.

If she possessed such things as determination and ingenuity, she thought with an uncomfortable frown.

Leaning back in the chair, she studied the ceiling for a while, her expression blank, her thoughts involved. And that was when she made the decision.

It was time for Rae to find out just exactly what she was made of.

Tanner walked slowly up the steps and opened the door. Then, instead of going inside, he turned and leaned against the doorjamb, looking out across the land.

His house, the place he had called home since he was sixteen years old, was a small, nondescript cabin at the very back of the McCallister property. Before moving here, he had stayed in a bedroom off the kitchen at the big house. It had taken him almost two months to convince Joe that he was old enough to live by himself, but eventually he had done it. Tanner could be just as stubborn as the old man when he wanted to be.

Nineteen years and Tanner still loved it out here. He loved the isolation, the uncluttered freedom. And most of the time the distant view, the view he was gazing at now, brought him a measure of peace.

But not tonight. Tonight the demons inside Tanner were running wild.

It happened sometimes. He would stand watching darkness grow across the land and would feel it growing inside him as well. Darkness and a hot, restless spirit that boiled through his insides.

When he was younger, he had used whiskey to chase the mood away, but it hadn't taken him long to figure out that alcohol merely made the bad times last longer. Riding it out was the only way.

He had intended to go up to the big house later for a poker game, but he knew he wouldn't. It would be better for everyone if he was alone tonight.

Turning away from the shadowy landscape, he closed the door behind him with a little shove and stripped off his shirt, dropping it on the floor as he headed for the shower.

It had been a long, hot, dusty day and the night didn't look as though it was getting any better.

Rae stepped from her car and stood looking across it toward the house. Then, drawing in a deep breath, she began to move, around the car, across the bare yard, and up three unpainted wooden steps.

At the door she hesitated, and several seconds passed before she finally straightened her back and raised her hand to knock.

At her first tap the wooden door swung open under her hand. Across the threshold, it was dark. Dark and silent. Empty. Tanner wasn't home.

A small laugh escaped her. For two solid hours she had been worrying, arguing silently, trying to build up enough courage to come out here. And now he wasn't home.

Leaning forward, she grasped the knob to pull the door shut. But somehow, when the door closed, she was on the wrong side, inside his house instead of on her way back to the car.

Rae had never been a nosy person. She held a great respect for the privacy of the individual, but there was something about being given the chance to inspect the lair of Dicton's lone wolf that was too compelling for her to resist.

The cabin was one big open space. Kitchen, dining room, sitting room, and bedroom all came together in a single living area. And although the sides were more window than wall, there was not a curtain to be seen. Unhampered moonlight silvered the area, giving relief from the darkness, hinting at mysterious shapes and surfaces.

The room was a mess. Clothes on the floor and on chairs. Newspapers scattered across the couch and falling off the massive stone coffee table. His bed—extra long, extra wide, and minus a head-board—was unmade, the cover hanging half on and

half off as though it had been flung impatiently aside.

Stacks of paperback books covered the top of
the bedside table and, moving closer, Rae picked
up one and held it to a stream of moonlight, curious to see what a man like Tanner West chose
to read.

Contrary to her expectations, the book she held
wasn't something with erotic illustrations. It was
Thomas Hardy's *Jude the Obscure*. And there were
Steinbeck, Thoreau, and Faulkner. Not a single—

In the next instant Rae's breath left her in a
soft *whoosh* as she was caught around the waist and
thrown back onto the bed.

When a solid weight settled on top of her, she
fought instinctively. With her heart pounding in her
ears and her breath coming in short gasps, she struggled wildly against the shadowy force that held her
down. And as she fought, as she pushed and twisted,
her hands came up against warm, damp flesh. Hard,
naked flesh.

Tanner was home after all.

"Lonely, Rae?" The words were a rasping whisper against her left ear. "Tired of dusty dreams? I
thought I wanted to be alone tonight." She felt his
laughter in the tips of her fingers, in her palms, and
on her cheek. "Just shows how a person never really
knows his own mind."

"Don't be an idiot," she said, breathless, as she continued to try to push him off her. "I came out here to—"

"—to visit the wicked side of life? Turnabout's fair play. I took a trip to the land of the good. Now you get to see how the other half lives. The half that goes to sleep satisfied." His voice grew even huskier as his lips brushed across the side of her neck. "Tell me your fantasies, Rae. Tell me and I'll make them happen."

When he shifted his position slightly, his lower body moved against hers, bringing a sharp twinge of awareness that surged through her, startling her.

"Tanner . . . get *off*!" she gasped.

He moved his chin in a rough caress at the base of her throat. "Or maybe it would be better if I helped you out. I don't want to hurt your feelings, Rae, but I'm afraid your fantasies might be a little on the dull side. How about I list the possibilities for you? All you have to do is stop me when I get to the one that turns you on."

Again silent laughter shook him. "Put your missionary-position past right out of your mind, sweetness, because tonight you're going to find out what it's all about. For starters, we could try an erotic little exercise I learned back when—"

Gathering all her strength, Rae pushed again, and suddenly, unexpectedly, she was free.

Scrambling from the bed, she began to straighten her blouse and smooth down her skirt. "This was a mistake," she muttered in irritation. "Why didn't I know it would be a mistake? But I did. Of course I did. I *knew* it was a mistake, and I came out here anyway. Of all the stupid—"

She broke off when the lamp beside the bed flashed on, momentarily blinding her.

As her eyes adjusted, she kept her gaze carefully away from him and glanced around the room. Surprisingly, beneath the clutter his house was clean. It was an attractive room, with cream walls and smooth lines to the furniture. But something was missing. Tanner's personality was missing. There were no pictures on the walls. No bric-a-brac or plants. Not even a dusty old artificial flower arrangement. There were none of the little personal touches that made a house a home. The cabin's living space had a temporary feel to it, as though the occupant were simply marking time until he could move back to where he really belonged.

Drawing in a slow breath, she turned her attention to Tanner. He was standing to the right and slightly behind her. She couldn't see him, but she knew he was there. She sensed it, the way a deer could sense the presence of a mountain lion.

Biting her lip, she dipped her head and shot a cautious glance in his direction.

He wasn't naked. At least not completely. He wore the usual faded jeans, but tonight the top three metal buttons were unfastened so that they hung dangerously low on his hips. Moving her gaze away from that disturbing triangle of flesh, she raised her head and found him studying her face.

"Well, that was fun," he said, the words slow and lazy. "But something tells me you didn't come all the way out here to provide entertainment for a tired man. So what's up?"

She wasn't quite as good at ignoring his bare skin as she had hoped. "Do up your jeans," she said shortly, glancing away from the sight of him.

"Too tempting?" He laughed as he fastened the buttons. "There, is that better? I'm afraid this is as decent as I get. And I repeat, what's up?"

It was time. This was what she had come here for. All she had to do was ask. All she had to do was say the words. If she could just manage to get the first few words out of her mouth, the rest would surely follow.

But she couldn't.

By pulling up hidden reserves, Rae had found the courage to make the decision, and she had found the courage to come out here, but when it came to actually saying the words aloud, she simply couldn't.

Shaking her head, she turned and walked toward the door. "Never mind. I'm sorry I barged in on you." She pulled the door open without looking at him. "Just forget I was here."

In the next moment she found her arm caught in an iron grasp. "Oh no, you don't," he said, swinging her back around as he slammed the door shut with one foot. "You can't come out here, disrupting my peaceful evening, and then say never mind."

He leaned against the door and folded his arms on his chest. "Besides, you've got me curious now. For the past two years you've spent most of your time avoiding me. So why did you go out of your way to track me down tonight?"

Exhaling a slow, careful breath, she brushed a curl from her forehead and glanced away from him. "Promise you won't tease me?"

"No." There was open amusement in his voice. "Teasing you is one of the few pleasures I have in life. You walked into my territory, now you have to pay the price. Tell me why you're here."

Moistening her lips, she edged sideways to put some distance between them. "You know how it is, sometimes when you're alone, and tired . . . and maybe dissatisfied with your life, your mind goes off in strange directions."

Suddenly impatient with her own cowardice, she raised her chin and said, "Most of what you say to me I manage to ignore. Because most of what you say to me is stupid, and I know that needling me . . .

amuses you. But there is one thing you said that I believe."

"Only one?" He raised a dark brow. "I must be slipping. I used to be a better liar than that."

"I believe that if anyone could teach me to be—" She broke off and cleared her throat again. "If anyone could teach me how to be hot, it's you."

Exhaling a slow breath, she raised her head and met his eyes. "Okay, now you can laugh."

But Tanner wasn't laughing. He wasn't even smiling. A frown etched deep creases between his dark brows as he stared at her.

A moment later he pushed away from the door and walked to a window near the bed. "You want me to—" He broke off and shook his head.

"In all fairness, you did make the offer," she reminded him stiffly. "It doesn't matter that you offered simply to annoy me. The fact is, if anyone can do it, you can." She moved her shoulders in a short shrug. "So that's why I'm here, to ask you if you'll teach me how to attract Drew's attention."

When he didn't respond, she slid damp palms over the sides of her skirt. "It should give you some satisfaction to know you were right about me. Except that what you call repression is really ignorance. I didn't have to learn how to grab a man's attention. I always had Johnny. From the time I was a little girl, I knew I was going to marry him. There was no need for teenage flirtations and things like that. I may be starting late, but I'm not stupid. I can learn . . . that is, if you'll agree to help me."

"Forget it." His voice was rough and emphatic, his face still turned toward the darkness outside. "Read a book, take a course, make friends with a call girl. But forget about me. I'm not the altruistic type."

She nodded slowly. "Okay . . . okay, that's fair. There's no reason why you should do me a favor. What do you think is a fair price?"

This got his attention. He turned to look at her, one dark brow raised in inquiry. "You want me to teach you how to be a woman," he said, his gaze sliding over her body. "And you're going to pay me to do it?"

He gave a short, almost soundless laugh and began to move toward her. "I'll have to give this some heavy thought. Definitely intriguing. I knew a guy once whose father took him to a hooker when he was sixteen. Said she would teach him to be a man. Interesting parallel, don't you think?"

She watched him silently, knowing that he was taunting her, that he was deliberately trying to antagonize her, but fascinated against her will by the seductive quality of his voice and the blatant sensuality in his movements as he slowly closed the distance between them.

Taking an involuntary step backward, she said, "I didn't mean to imply that you . . . well, that you—"

"Could be bought?" he suggested as he moved even closer. "That's exactly what you meant to imply. And as it happens, you were right. Under certain circumstances, I can be bought."

"Tanner, this is ridiculous. Just—"

She broke off when she backed into the door. A moment later, as his eyes caught and held hers, he reached out and unfastened the wide clip at the back of her neck. Although Rae caught her breath in surprise, she did nothing to stop him. She simply stood staring into his eyes as he ran his fingers through her hair, loosening it, freeing the curls.

"Oh yes." The words were low and husky. "I will definitely have to give this more thought."

He was trying to make her angry. He was playing with her again so that she would lose her temper and lash out at him as she had always done in the past. But it didn't happen. Instead of anger, his touch brought a different response.

When Tanner freed her hair, she felt as though other things were being freed as well. Things inside her. Secret things.

This man was a danger to her. The thought came to her from nowhere, so forceful that she felt stupid for not having seen it before.

She didn't like Tanner, but liking him wasn't necessary. She had a goal, and he was just the man to help her achieve it. He would teach her a few superficial tricks, tell her what she was doing wrong. Only then would she be able to attract Drew and take the first step toward having the family she so desperately wanted.

She had never even stopped to consider the possibility that Tanner might reach places inside her that no one had ever reached before. Not even Johnny.

"I'll do it."

The words broke abruptly into her thoughts, and she glanced quickly around the room.

He had moved again and now stood several feet away from her, outside the light thrown by the single lamp, but even though she couldn't see him clearly, she could still feel the heat of his intense concentration.

Blinking in confusion, she said, "I beg your pardon?"

"I said I'll do it. I'll teach you how to use your natural ability. Show you what it takes to get a man to notice you. And there will be no charge."

"Oh." The word was hesitant, slightly breath-less.

This was what she wanted, what she had come here to accomplish. But his sudden about-face took her off-guard. Compliance from Tanner made her extremely nervous.

"Why?" she asked, unable to keep the suspicion from her voice. "What do you get out of it? What do you want from me in return?"

He didn't answer immediately. Layers of shadow still obscured his features, and she had only the impression of dark, deep-set eyes trained on her with such fierce strength that it made her knees weak.

The silence drew out, hanging heavily in the air between them. And then, from out of the darkness, came two roughly whispered words. *"Your soul."*

The hair on the back of Rae's neck stood on end, and her heart gave a skittering sideways leap.

And then she realized he was laughing.

She waited, tapping one foot, her arms crossed, her lips tight, while he leaned against the window and laughed.

When he finally straightened again, he wiped his eyes with the backs of his hands and shook his head. "You should have seen your face," he said, his voice unsteady with leftover laughter.

"Very funny."

"Yes, it was. Very funny. You, and half the town along with you, think I'm in league with the Devil." He grinned. "I thought I'd give you a little of what you expected."

Annoying, aggravating, intolerable man. If she had to see him on a regular basis, he would probably drive her crazy. But it was a chance Rae would have to take. She had made a decision, and she wouldn't back down. She was going to go after what she wanted.

"So what's the real reason you're going to help me?" she asked, studying his face.

He had moved to sit on the bed. Now, leaning against the wall, he rested his hands loosely on bent knees and stared straight ahead, his face again in shadows.

"I want Lynda," he said, the words blunt. "And since I can't go after a woman Drew is interested in, this little deal will kill two birds with one stone. You get your hero, and I inherit the blond bombshell."

He laughed. "Talk about an unholy alliance. What we've got here is a symbiotic union of good and evil."

As he turned his head toward her, his lips moved in a strange, twisted smile. "You use me, I use you . . . and we both get what we want."

FOUR

It was an ordinary summer Saturday. The sky was bright blue, just as usual. The sun glinted off the water of Lake Ed Briscoe the way it always did in the summer. Ski boats and cabin cruisers sped by, leaving behind big waves that grew smaller and smaller until only a tiny bit of motion remained to touch the shore.

The laws of nature still applied.

On a faded quilt beneath a large pin oak, Rae and Glenna sat cross-legged as they watched the latter's nieces, three-year-old twins, throw sticks and small pebbles into the water. Also a perfectly natural scene.

But in some strange morning-after-the-night-before effect, Rae felt disconnected from the normality all around her. It didn't seem right that the world could still be so sane when Rae herself had gone around the bend.

Swallowing a groan, she closed her eyes and lay back on the quilt. She had actually done it. Last night she had gone to Tanner West, the one man in the world guaranteed to set her teeth on edge, and asked him to teach her how to attract a man's attention.

Had this small gap in her sanity always been there, she wondered now, just waiting for her to stumble across it? Or was it some symptom of having lived alone for so long? Maybe this was the first step toward turning into one of those sweet old women who wore outrageous hats and a bathrobe while they talked to invisible friends.

"For heaven's sake, what is wrong with you?"

Opening her eyes, she found Glenna frowning as she stared sideways at her. "Sorry," Rae said, sitting up. "Did you say something?"

"I've been saying and saying all morning, but you haven't heard a word. You keep muttering to yourself and exhaling those breathy little moans. It's damned weird. I told you not to sit up with Miss Rodale's electric bills last night. Those things would put anyone in a blue funk."

Rae brushed an ant off the quilt, bit her lip, and shot a hesitant glance at her friend. "Can I ask you something?"

"Uh-uh." The brunette started shaking her head. "Not if you're going to ask me to take over those bills. Charts and graphs give me gas."

"Forget Miss Rodale for a minute." She paused and rubbed her forehead with the tip of one finger as she tried to gather her thoughts. "I want to ask you a hypothetical question. What if . . . Okay, what if you were interested in a man—"

"That's no great stretch. There are a few dozen men I'm interested in."

"But what if there were only one. Just imagine you were single because you chose to be—"

"My imagination's not that good."

"—because you were waiting for a certain kind of man. An exceptional man. The only kind of man you wanted to be the father of your children."

"I get to have children in this hypothetical question? I don't know, Rae, do you really think I'd make a good mother? How many kids are we talking about?"

"Will you shut up and let me get to the question!" Clamping her mouth shut, Rae closed her eyes and counted to ten.

"Okay," she said a few moments later, forcing calm into her voice. "Now what if you found the kind of man you'd been looking for, but he didn't find you? I mean, what if you really wanted this man, but he barely knew you were alive?"

Glenna scratched her knee, her eyes narrowed in thought. "In the first place, the kind of man you're talking about, good father material, isn't the kind of man I'd ever have sweaty dreams over. But if something weirdly hormonal happened and I found myself seriously attracted to this *Father Knows Best* type, I don't know, I guess I'd chase him down and sit on him until he liked me back."

Rae made a soft sound of exasperation. "Why do I talk to you?"

"Because the twins are in the water, and I'm all that's left." Glenna glanced enviously at the two little girls, who had shed their clothes and were now splashing in the shallow water. "Let's go for it, Rae. Let's strip down to our silky drawers and go in with the girls."

"Right," Rae said, her tone sarcastic as she flopped back and closed her eyes again. "And give Mickey E. apoplexy."

Michael Edward Dawson, the park ranger, known as Mickey E. in order to distinguish him from his father, Mickey G., hauled people before the justice of the peace for dropping a candy wrapper on the grass. He wouldn't take kindly to his serene kingdom being thrown into disorder by two women in their skivvies.

"You have a chicken heart, Rae."

Rae was silent for a moment. "You know, I'm beginning to think you're right," she said with a small sigh.

Yesterday in her office when she had reached her momentous decision, it had seemed so clear-cut. So emphatically right. She would go after what she wanted. Instead of letting the tides of fate sweep her along, she would swim like hell and go in the direction of her choice.

Even at the cabin, when she realized how incredible the idea sounded when spoken aloud, she had suppressed her natural doubts and convinced herself that desperate situations called for desperate measures. She had soothed her qualms with the thought that she was being determined and ingenious.

Now, in the clear light of day, she realized her determination and ingenuity were nothing more than self-delusions, a nice way of saying she had been stubbornly bizarre. Rae simply wasn't the type of person to scheme and maneuver. She couldn't blatantly—

"There she is again," Glenna said suddenly.

Keeping her eyes closed, Rae shook her head vehemently. "I don't want to see Lynda today," she said through clenched teeth. "I don't want to see Lynda or Paula who works at Beatty's, and I especially don't want to see Tanner."

"Tanner's not with them. It's just Drew and Miss Sexy Snotnose in the little sailboat. *They're looking this way*," Glenna hissed urgently. "Wave, Rae."

Rae sat up and shaded her eyes, looking out toward the open lake. The sailboat was skimming across the water, fifty yards or so off the bank. Drew, in white shorts and blue polo shirt, looked tanned and fit, the sun picking up the blond streaks in his hair. When he yelled a greeting and waved at them, Rae waved back.

Lynda didn't wave. She was too busy looking sexy. The blonde had exchanged the thong bikini for a sleek black swimsuit, cut to the pubic bone in front and nothing but crisscrossed strings on the side. Hot enough to make a man's eyes sting.

Rae, on the other hand, was wearing khaki shorts, a pink camp shirt, and pink tennis shoes, her auburn hair pulled up in a ponytail and held by a pink elastic band.

Seventy-six degrees, tops.

"She's probably dumb as a post," Glenna muttered, squinting her eyes against the sun.

"Maybe, but Drew hasn't noticed. Or if he's noticed, he obviously doesn't consider it a drawback." Rae rose abruptly to her feet. "I'm going to walk up to the marina for a magazine. Do you want anything?"

"Yeah, bring me one of those cookie, caramel, chocolate-covered things . . . and two of those little chocolate sodas . . . and a bag of cheese twists— What's that look for? Would you like to make a comment about my eating habits? When *you're* depressed, you do something energetic. I eat. Different metabolism. And get me some sugarless gum!" she yelled after her departing friend.

As Rae walked along the gravel road, she rubbed at a stain on her shorts. Khaki walking shorts, she thought, rolling her eyes in contempt. Birdwatcher's gear.

But, of course, her clothes had never been the issue. Even if she had a swimsuit like Lynda's, she wouldn't be able to make it a part of her personality the way the blonde did.

What was it Tanner had said? *Hot's not on the surface. It's how you handle what's inside you.* Rae frowned. Was there anything inside her? What if along with her birdwatcher's clothes, she also had birdwatcher's sexuality?

Making love with Johnny had been wonderful, like being wrapped in a cocoon of security and warmth, but neither of them had placed an inordinate amount of importance on sex. It was simply another way of expressing their love for each other. It was a way of reaffirming their closeness.

Wildfire.

Tanner said he had seen wildfire in her. But surely Rae should know better than anyone what was inside her. And never once had she felt anything remotely resembling that kind of heat.

Warm and cozy was the best she would ever do, she told herself with a resigned sigh as she turned onto the main road that led to the marina.

Sandridge Marina was one of three marinas on Lake Ed Briscoe, and the only one that didn't cater exclusively to fishermen. Along with several rows of boat stalls there were a general store, a gas pump, and a small café that always smelled of stale grease.

Bypassing the café, Rae stepped into the store and gave a small sigh as the refrigerated air hit her. Living up to its name, the general store kept in stock all the things you were sure to forget on a trip to the lake. Suntan lotion and insect repellent. Potato chips and charcoal briquettes. Silly bumper stickers and cheap sunglasses.

After pulling a cold drink from the cooler, she headed for the magazine rack at the back of the store and began to browse through the surprisingly large selection.

"The Sexiest Summer Clothes Ever."

"How to Keep a Man Happy . . . and at Home."

"Has Your Mate Stopped Enjoying Sex?"

"What Do Men *REALLY* Want . . . The Revealing Results of Our Nationwide Survey."

In self-defense Rae grabbed a news magazine and began to thumb through it, searching frantically for something that had nothing to do with men or sex. As she was trying to get seriously interested in an article about a labor bill that was doomed to be vetoed, Lynda and Drew walked into the store.

Stifling a long-suffering groan, Rae slowly raised the magazine until it covered her face. Of all the things she didn't need at the moment, running into Drew and Lynda was at the top of the list. Today, with Rae in crumpled clothes and her hair damp with perspiration, the contrast between her and the blonde would be just too depressing.

"I thought that was you."

Jumping in startled reaction, Rae slowly lowered the magazine.

Drew was standing a couple of feet away, smiling that wonderful smile at her. A smile that said that running into her was one of life's little unexpected pleasures. The same smile he gave to the mayor's wife and to Glenna and to any stranger he happened to pass on the street.

"Hi," she said, returning his smile with a twitch of her lips. She glanced behind him. "Where's your friend?"

Motioning toward the ladies' room, he examined her face with a soft chuckle. "Your nose is getting pink. You'd better watch it, Rae. Say, why don't you come out with us for a while? I have some sunscreen on the boat. And enough food for an army if you're hungry. Mrs. Tease baked a wonderful chocolate-cherry cake."

She shook her head. "Thanks anyway, but Glenna and I have her two nieces with us, and I don't think—"

"Drew?"

The word, spoken in a breathy and slightly petulant way, gained his immediate attention. Lynda stood by the entrance, her head tilted to the side, her lower lip drooping in a sensual moue of discontent.

"See you around, Rae," Drew said with an absentminded wave as he walked away.

On the half-mile trip back to the cove where she had left Glenna and the girls, Rae paused occasionally to pick up a rock and throw it at a tree or a sign or a bush. She rarely hit anything, but once she had the satisfaction of scaring some ducks.

As she walked, she muttered, "Slop some sunscreen on her nose . . . feed her chocolate-cherry cake . . . take her for a ride in the nice sailboat. Like somebody's kid sister."

It wasn't fair. Rae was what she was. She didn't want to wear peekaboo swimsuits and talk in breathless, pouting tones. She didn't want to pretend to be something she wasn't. She didn't want—

Suddenly, interrupting her thought processes, came a picture of the twins with their chubby bodies and silly smiles. Their grubby kisses and exuberant hugs.

Rae drew in a sharp breath. Sweet heaven, she wanted that. She wanted to hold her own babies. She wanted to bathe them and read stories to them and rock them to sleep. She wanted to give them all the love she had inside her. The love that was just sitting there, going to waste. The love that ached to be given away.

Wiping away unbidden tears, Rae straightened her shoulders and started walking again.

When she reached the inlet, the twins were sleeping, and Glenna was stretched out beside them on the quilt, her eyes closed.

Rae stood staring down at the little girls for a long time; then, switching her gaze to the brunette, she nudged Glenna with the tip of one foot. There was no immediate response, so she nudged again, then again and again, putting more force behind it each time.

"What? *What?*" Glenna sat up and shaded her eyes to look up at Rae. "What?" she repeated.

"I want you to cut my hair."

Rae began to pace back and forth beside the quilt, wrapping the hair at her temples around her fingers and giving it sharp little tugs. "When we get home, I want you to cut my hair for me. Do you hear me? And it's got to be a drastic change. I want you to give me a look that's not even in the same room with wholesome."

"What's got into you? Where's my chocolate, my cheese twists?" Glenna's eyes narrowed in suspicion. "Have you been drinking? *What* have you been drinking?" She glanced around. "Is Petey DuPuy selling that homemade stuff out of the back of his truck again?"

"I haven't been drinking, but I might start." Rae leaned against the rough trunk of the oak tree, then pushed away again, unable to keep still. "I'm going to make some changes, Glenna. No more lukewarm. You were right. Chase 'em down and sit on 'em. I'm not going to wait around for someone to hand me what I want. I'm going to go out and get it . . . no matter what I have to do."

She would see Tanner tonight to start her lessons. And she would get hot or die trying.

Rae was sitting on the steps, her chin resting in the palms of her hands, when Tanner walked around the corner of the cabin, coming from the direction of the stables. Although his shirt was only half-buttoned, allowing altogether too much of his tanned chest to show, he was fully dressed.

Somehow, it seemed like a good omen.

Stopping short at the sight of her, he raised one dark brow, then stepped past her to open the door.

"So you really showed up." He stood aside to let her follow him inside. "I didn't think you would. I figured you would start thinking, and with you, that's always a mistake."

"Funny," she said, her voice dry.

He closed the door behind her and leaned against it. Silently and with great concentration, he studied her hair. As the examination drew out, Rae stared at the ceiling and tapped her foot with impatience.

"Definitely an improvement," he said finally. "You freed up the curls. Pert. Sassy."

With a movement that caught her off-guard, he reached out and removed one of the combs that held back the sides of the chin-length bob. Spiral curls sprang forward to almost cover her right eye.

"Now you could even call it flirty. You look like a woman of the nineties. Just exactly the right blend of practical and sexy."

"I'm so glad you approve," she said, the words sarcastic as she pretended to ignore the possessive satisfaction in his husky voice. "I worried all day about whether or not you would like it."

"I'm in charge of this project," he said. "And that means my word is law. If I hadn't liked it, you would've had to do something else."

Biting back a sharp retort, she drew in a deep breath and let it slide. She had a feeling there were going to be a lot of things she would have to let slide before this was over.

After a moment she moved on into the room and turned to face him. "Okay, so where do we start?"

"Right there."

She glanced behind her. "Right where?"

"The way you talk. Blunt. To the point. Exploratory conversation hasn't got a chance with you. It's get in, get it over with, and get out. You've got to soften up a little. Start with a few minor forays. Tease a little. Hint at deeper mysteries to come. Leave a man with the impression that there's more to you than meets the eye."

She let out a huffing breath of air. "I have no mysteries. How can I hint at what I don't have? I can't even pretend to have it, because I don't know what it is I'm supposed to have . . . of which I definitely don't have any!"

He cocked his head to one side and gave her a glance. "A little heavy on the frustration. We'll have to work on that."

By the time she finished counting, he had moved to the couch and was pushing a scattering of newspapers aside. "Come over here and sit down," he said, glancing over his shoulder. "We might as well get started."

When she was settled on the couch, he dropped down beside her, flinging one arm over the back as he turned sideways to study her.

"Uncross your arms," he ordered abruptly. "That's a defensive move. It tells people you want to keep them out. The point is to invite them in. Or in this case, invite him in."

She shot him a belligerent look. "Do you have to criticize everything I do?"

"Yes." His tone was firm and implacable. "That's my job. Okay, the first thing you have to understand is that I'm not going to teach you how to be hot."

Her head came up abruptly. "But you said—"

"Calm down. I told you from the very first that you had all the stuff you need. You just don't know how to share it with the rest of the world. With a pint of bourbon under your belt, you'd probably turn it loose, but you can't very well go around snockered all the time."

He leaned back and smiled. "And that's where I come in. I'm going to show you what you've got, then teach you how to use it."

She sent him a skeptical look. "Wouldn't it be easier if I just faked it?"

He shook his head. "That would be like faking orgasm, only it'd last longer. You couldn't keep it up. Some women maybe, but not you. You'd know you were faking, which means so would everyone else. I never met a more honest face."

"I never faked—" She broke off and drew in a slow breath. "Okay, so where do we—" She broke off again and clamped her mouth shut. She was already back to blunt.

He chuckled. "You don't have to watch every word. That's what I'm trying to tell you. When you free up the inner stuff, the rest comes automatically."

Rubbing the tip of her nose with one finger, Rae cut her eyes toward him. She hadn't known what to expect tonight, but she had to give credit where credit was due. He seemed to have given this some thought. And what he said made sense.

How she hated making that admission, even to herself.

Nodding reluctantly, she said, "Okay, I see your point, but I still don't understand how you're going to do it."

The glittering amusement in his eyes acknowledged her lingering wariness. "We'll take it slow, maybe work on your reactions to a man in a casual situation, do some loosening-up exercises. You need to get to know me first, get used to being around me."

When he reached up to touch one of the newly freed curls, she stiffened.

"You see?" he said.

There had been no change in his tone as he touched her hair. No intimacy had been added to his voice. It was sensual, but Tanner's voice was naturally sensual, constantly sensual. It was one of the things about him that had always disturbed her.

She cleared her throat. "See what?"

"You see how fast your guard goes up? We're going to have to knock that down first of all. Wipe it out. You have to learn to relax around me."

Avoiding his eyes, she shifted her position and pulled her hair free of his teasing fingers. "Why do I need to relax around you? Drew is the one—"

"Forget Drew for right now." The words were abrupt, almost harsh. "This isn't about him. It's about you. And I can't teach you about yourself until you trust me enough to listen and learn."

Once again his perception took her by surprise. "All right, I guess that sounds reasonable."

He gave a soft laugh. "You don't have to sound so shocked. You came to me because you knew I could get the job done. Didn't you?"

"I suppose I did," she admitted grudgingly.

"Right, now where were we?"

"I'm supposed to learn how to relax around you."

He nodded. "You learn to relax, and then we work on opening your mind to new experiences."

"New experiences," she echoed, her tone absorbed as she began to take mental notes.

"I've noticed that you always think before you speak, before you act. You spend most of your time counting to ten, and all that does is inhibit your natural responses. You're going to have to learn how to be more spontaneous. You have to be completely at ease with yourself before you'll be able to follow through on an instinctive reaction."

Again she nodded. "And then?"

He tilted his head back and rubbed his chin, his eyes narrowed in thought. "And then . . . this is just off the top of my head, you understand, I haven't got a schedule mapped out or anything, but next we would probably want to get naked and jump in bed for a couple of days."

Several seconds ticked by before the words sank in, and she grasped what he said. Then she was on her feet, shaking with fury as she stood before him.

He had done it to her again.

"You—I should have known!" She scooped up a magazine from the floor and threw it at him, then another and another. "Dammit, I should have known! You are the most—Every time I—Oh, *go screw yourself*!"

She was out the door and halfway across the yard when she heard his belated response.

"By George, I think we're making progress."

• • •

Rae had flipped through all the television channels twice before she realized what she was doing. Punching the buttons for the PBS station, she drew her legs up beside her and tucked the edges of the pink-striped nightshirt around her bare legs.

She wasn't in the mood for the dining habits of the little brown desert lizard. But then she wasn't in the mood for television, period, so it didn't really matter what was on the screen.

Exhaling a heavy sigh, she reluctantly admitted that the fiasco at Tanner's house two nights earlier had left her stuck in some awkward, purgatorial stage. She couldn't go back to being satisfied with the way things were, yet she couldn't move forward without his help.

And hell would freeze over before she'd give Tanner West another chance to make a fool of her.

If she had once stopped to think, she would have known she couldn't trust him. He was the town outlaw. Dicton's dark desperado. He had spent his whole life breaking the rules, along with a few noses and more than a few hearts. Only an idiot would have gone to him for help.

There had to be some other way, she told herself now. Maybe she could find out what committees Drew was on and sign up. With a little prolonged contact, she could impress him with her . . . what? Her civic-mindedness?

Brilliant.

She would be better off studying the fashion magazines, making a few subtle changes to match her new hairstyle. She wouldn't do anything blatant. That would make her feel self-conscious, and everyone would know she was pretending to be something she wasn't. Tanner had been right about that. But a little store-bought sex appeal couldn't hurt anything. She would drive to Dallas for a weekend of shopping and—

At that moment a noise from her bedroom reached her, putting an end to all thought. It was a sliding sound, the kind a window makes when it's being closed. Or opened.

As her heart began beating a rapid tattoo, she glanced around in panic, then slipped off the couch and crept toward the hearth. Picking up the bronze cat that had been a wedding present from Johnny's great-aunt Flora, she tiptoed down the hall to the bedroom door and silently eased it open.

She held the cat by its long, slender neck, raised it slowly above her head, and reached in to flick on the overhead light.

"The police are on the way, so you'd better not—" Breaking off abruptly, she stood and stared, her eyes slowly widening in disbelief.

Tanner was kneeling on the window seat, his back turned to her as he closed her bedroom window.

"I don't believe it." The words were a blend of anger and relief. "You really are incredible. Is there some reason why you can't use the front door like ordinary people? Are the old criminal tendencies catching up with you again?"

"Rae, Rae." He shook his head in a slow, regretful movement. "I'm surprised at you. I thought you were too morally upright to listen to gossip spread around by—"

He broke off and raised one brow as he examined her. Slowly, giving consideration to each detail. Starting at her feet, moving up her long legs, lingering at her high breasts before going on to her disheveled hair.

"I have just revised my opinion of candy-striped cotton nightshirts." The hoarse, gravelly sound of his voice sounded even more provocative than usual.

Resisting the urge to pull at the hem of her nightshirt, she placed the bronze cat on the bureau; then, drawing in a slow breath, she turned to face him. "Tanner," she said sweetly, "why did you crawl through my bedroom window?"

"Gossip again. I know what people would say if they saw the notorious Tanner West calling on Dicton's resident nun in the middle of the night.

It would get you some attention, but not the kind you want."

After a moment she nodded. "I'll accept that. But it doesn't explain why you're here at all."

"You missed your appointment two nights in a row." He turned over his right hand and began to examine his fingernails. "I was afraid I had, you know, inadvertently said something to offend you. I know how sensitive you are, and I'd hate for you to get the wrong idea."

She reacted with an inelegant snort. "I'm sure regret is just eating you alive. You knew very well I wouldn't be back. You did it on purpose. I came to you, seriously asking for your help, and you—"

"And I was seriously giving you my help."

With that careless dismissal, he began moving about her room, his gaze exploring her private world. A moment later he picked up a snow-white lace-edged pillow and held it to his face, inhaling the scent.

"I recognize that," he murmured. "I catch a hint of it any time you're around. What is it?" The question was not directed at her, but at some piece of his own memory. "Tropical flowers and seafoam? A mermaid's hair would smell like this."

Glancing over his shoulder, he finally returned his attention to Rae. "I got a reaction out of you, didn't I?"

She pulled the pillow out of his hand and dropped it back to the bed. "I didn't come to you to learn how to lose my temper. After two years of being in the same town with you, I'm getting pretty good at it."

Her last words were directed at his back because he had moved past her to stand in front of her dressing table. He picked up a sable brush and feathered it across his lips, then dropped it and began to examine an eyeliner pencil.

"I can never remember if mascara is the tube thing or the pencil thing."

When he started to remove the glass stopper from her perfume, Rae stepped forward and snatched the bottle from his hand. "Will you please stick to the point?"

He switched his gaze to her face and smiled, obviously amused by her frustration. "You do it. Lawyers are trained point stickers, so why don't you take over?"

"Okay, I will," she said tightly. "And the point is, our 'unholy alliance,' as you call it, won't work. We would end up killing each other. You rub me the wrong way, and I—Don't you dare make something suggestive out of that," she warned when he opened his mouth to speak. "You know what I mean. How can I accomplish anything if I'm always mad at you?"

"Who says you'll always be mad at me?" He leaned his hip against the dressing table. "You never know, I might start to grow on you." He tilted his head slightly, one brow raised. "I can be awfully winsome when I put my mind to it."

At that moment Rae discovered it was possible to be furiously angry and at the same time feel the overpowering urge to laugh.

Clearing her throat noisily, she moved to sit on the edge of the bed.

"I don't think so," she said finally. "I'm sure you can be as charming as all get-out when you try. There are enough women mooning over you to tell me you have something. But the thing is, you're never charming to *me*. Not that I want you to be charming," she added quickly. "You know what I mean. You and I simply don't get along."

"Coward."

"I'm not—"

"Yes, you are. You're a wuss. I knew it all along. You haven't got the intestinal fortitude of a limp piece of parsley."

"Courage has nothing to do with this."

"Sure it does. Do you have the guts to go after what you want? Or maybe the real question is, is Drew really what you want? If you're not willing to put up with me for a little while to get him, he can't be all that important to you."

She gritted her teeth. "Why are you pushing, Tanner?"

His lips stretched in a slow, sensual smile that made her want to smack his face. "Lynda is still out there, and she's still got enough sizzle to melt a Hershey bar from fifty yards away. How am I ever going to get a shot at her if you give up now?"

"That's not my problem."

"I think Drew's losing interest in her." He leaned toward her, his voice low and tempting. "He must have gotten a good look inside the cereal box. Now would be the perfect time for you to make your move, before he goes hunting again and comes home with another one just like her."

Frowning, she studied the devilish gleam in his dark eyes. "If she can't hold Drew's interest any longer than that, why do you want her?"

He moved his shoulders in a brief shrug. "Different requirements. Drew thinks a meal should have meat and potatoes as well as dessert. Not me. Just hand me the pie and a fork and I'm happy. Come to think of it, forget the fork. I can—"

"Do you really think he's losing interest?"

"He came out to work with the men today while the lovely Lynda lay all alone by the pool . . . and you should have seen the bathing suit she was almost wearing today." He gave a low whistle at the memory.

Rae caught her bottom lip between her teeth. Maybe Tanner was right. If Lynda had really spent the entire day alone, it wouldn't be unreasonable to assume that Drew was having second thoughts about the relationship. Maybe now—

A sudden shiver shook through Rae, and she let out a helpless little moan.

"What kind of face is that?" he asked. "You look like you just found half a worm in your apple."

"Something like that," she said wryly. "I think hell's about to freeze over."

She gave him a cautious look and rose to her feet. "You promise you won't make any more lewd remarks?"

With a low, husky laugh he shook his head. "Sorry, I can't do that. Your definition of lewd is different from mine. How about I promise not to suggest a couple of days in bed again? Will that put your timid little soul at ease?"

She rubbed her knuckles across her chin, glancing at him from the corners of her eyes. She didn't trust him. She didn't trust him for a minute. But she wanted Drew.

"I'm out of my mind," she muttered. "Brain-dead. Over the edge and out of sight." She drew in a slow breath. "Okay, I'll do it."

He grinned and walked to the window seat. "I knew you'd come around," he said as he raised the window. "It's the dimple in my chin. Gets 'em every time."

After she had fastened the window behind him, after watching him vault over her back fence, Rae sat down on the window seat and closed her eyes, shaking her head slowly.

She was going to put herself in Tanner's hands.

God help her.

FIVE

"Okay," Tanner said, "it's time to get serious."

Rae, dressed in white slacks and a crisp peach-colored blouse, sat on the couch and stared warily at the man standing in front of her. For the past few days she had spent all her free time with him, trying, as he had told her she must, to feel at ease in his company.

Although "at ease" was a state of mind not to be found in proximity to Tanner, at least her hackles no longer rose automatically whenever he walked into sight.

She still couldn't claim she understood him. She doubted anyone really understood him. Trying to know Tanner was like trying to know a summer storm. Just when you got used to the torrential rain, you realized there was still more to come.

Wind and hail. Thunder and lightning. And that occasional burst of brilliant sunshine that sometimes broke through the clouds and always managed to take your breath away.

There were times when Rae would catch a glimpse of the moody wildness in his eyes. And there were times when, for no apparent reason, he would snap at her in anger. But more often than not, he made her laugh. Tanner had an unconventional, irreverent view of the world and all its rules, and he wasn't shy about sharing it.

"Get serious?" She said now as she shifted her position on the couch. "I'm not sure I like the sound of that. It makes me feel like I'm about to enter the Olympic tryouts."

"Did I ask for your opinion? Close your eyes."

She drew back her head in narrow-eyed suspicion. "What are you going to do? If you thump me on the head one more time, I swear I'll—"

"Close your eyes!"

Exhaling a small, irritated breath, she closed her eyes and waited. She didn't know what she was waiting for, but she was pretty sure she wouldn't like it.

"I don't trust you," she muttered. "I do *not* trust you, Tanner West."

A moment later, when she felt something soft against her face, her eyelids fluttered in surprise.

"Keep your eyes closed," he ordered as the softness began to move across her cheek.

"Am I supposed to guess what it is?" Her brows drew together in concentration. "It's silk. A scarf?"

"This isn't a guessing game." He must have been standing behind the couch, because his voice came from slightly above her. "You're supposed to feel it."

"I feel it."

"I said *feel* it, Rae." His voice was closer now, more intense. "Put everything else out of your mind and concentrate on the softness, move against it."

Muttering under her breath, she tilted her head to the side, allowing the silky softness to slide lower.

"That's right, but don't just feel it on your skin, feel it all the way through you. Sensual doesn't mean tight skirts and low-cut blouses. It means you revel in the senses. Touch, taste, smell, they all bring pleasure." His voice had dropped, and the low, husky words were a brush of warmth against her ear. "And touch is the most important of all."

Something was definitely happening, she decided silently. As she listened to his voice, coils of tension inside her began to slowly unwind, and her body became caught up in an exquisitely subtle languor.

Either I'm being hypnotized, she thought when her head fell lazily back against the couch, or my first serious involvement in nine years is going to be with a piece of fabric.

As her breathing grew slower and deeper, everything in her was given over to the feel of the silk, and she found herself savoring the slick softness as it moved against her cheek, whispered across her lips, and slid ever so slowly down her throat.

When Tanner spoke again, his voice was the merest trace of sound. "I want you to be aware of textures. As soon as you open yourself up to the sensation, you won't need anything as substantial as silk."

In a process she couldn't begin to explain, the low huskiness of his voice and the slippery softness of the silk began to merge, a bonding of sensations, a coupling of textures, until it was impossible to tell where one left off and the other began.

"Your skin will become responsive to even the most insubstantial touch," he whispered. "You'll feel the blood moving through your veins and the hidden vibrations of the earth. When you walk across a room, you'll feel the air stroking your body like an old, familiar lover. But you won't ever take the sensations for granted; you won't let them simply slide over and around you. You'll absorb them, Rae. You'll open all the warm, hidden places and let them in."

Exhaling a soft sigh, she arched her back slightly, luxuriating in the sound of his voice and the feel of the silk, twin pleasures that had magically become one.

As her sigh faded away, silence spread throughout the room, spilling into every crevice and corner with an almost solid presence.

And then, from somewhere behind her, Tanner cleared his throat loudly. "Okay, I think you're getting the idea."

Rae blinked a couple of times, opened her eyes, and sat up straighter. "That was amazing." Her voice was throaty and soft with awe. "I always thought silk was considered sexy because of the way it looks, putting the sexiness in the observer. I never thought about the way it makes you feel when you're wearing it . . . the way you react to the silk against your skin. Every time you move, you would feel it stroking your—"

"Right, right," he broke in, his voice short as he walked around the end of the couch. "Let's move on to something else now."

"But I'm excited." He had told her he would free up her inner substance, and that was exactly what he was doing. "I'm really learning something. I've worn silk hundreds of times, but I only ever paid attention to how it looked. Why do suppose that is? How did you know—"

"Enough with the silk already!" he snapped in

one of his abrupt, incomprehensible mood changes. "I wanted you to be aware of your senses. You're aware. Now we can move on to the next step."

"Which is?"

He pushed a rough hand through his hair and glanced at her. "What?"

She let out a short huff of exasperation. "I don't know what I did to set you off, or for that matter, if it was even something I did. From what I've learned of you in our cockeyed covenant, you can get seriously irate if the sun hits you from the wrong angle."

His lips tightened, his dark eyes flaring at the indictment. "So what's your point?"

"No point." She smiled. "I just wanted to get your attention so we could go on to the next step."

His features relaxed as he gave a low chuckle. "You think you're cute, don't you?" He raised one brow. "Cockeyed covenant?"

She grinned. "Don't complain, I almost said fet-id federation. Sometimes the pull of alliteration is too strong for me to resist."

"Try harder," he suggested. "Okay, next we're going to work on the way you look at a man."

"What's wrong with the way I look at men?" Now it was her turn to be irate. "I look at men just like every—"

"I didn't say men," he broke in. "I said man. One man in particular. You treat everyone the same.

Like people. Old Lady Evans or Drew, you make no distinction. You meet their eyes squarely, your expression open and honest, not a subtle invitation in sight. Which may be an asset for Ms. Anderson, ace lawyer, but its's a definite liability for the woman who wants to get her guy."

Although she wanted to argue the point, the honesty he was so quick to disparage wouldn't let her. Because his description of how she dealt with people, Drew included, was right on the money, damn him.

"Get over there by the window," he said, leaning down to push an armchair out of the way. "I'll start at this end of the room. We're going to walk toward each other like we're about to pass on the street."

Moving to the window, she stood with her hands clasped behind her back. "Why is it when someone's watching, you can never figure out what to do with your hands?"

"Oh, for Pete's sake," he snapped in irritation. "Pick up a magazine and pretend it's your briefcase. Nobody ever sees you without it anyway. Okay, start walking. As we get closer, which in reality would be probably, say, a quarter of a block away, you give me the once-over. Start at my feet and work your way up."

She gave him a look. "And in your world, this passes for subtle?"

"Since you think subtle is the same as hiding behind a bush, we'll go with my definition. Look, I'm not telling you to get a horny gleam in your eyes while you stare at his button fly. There shouldn't even be anything suggestive in the look. What you're doing is assessing this particular man as a possible mate."

"I feel silly," she muttered, then seeing his expression added, "I'll do it . . . but I still feel silly."

Clutching the magazine to her chest with one hand, she began to walk toward him. When she was a couple of yards away, she dropped her gaze to the scuffed, aged boots that showed below the jeans and began working her way up.

She managed his legs without too much difficulty, but when she reached his hips, Rae had to fight the urge to look away, knowing he would make fun of her if she did.

The soft, faded denim stretched across his slim hips and flat stomach like a fine kid glove, molding every muscle, every concave and convex curve, every single—

Feeling slightly flushed, she quickly left the button fly behind and raised her gaze to his chest. Today he wore an old blue work shirt. With more thought to comfort than fashion, the sleeves had been cut away completely, leaving his arms bare. Not a single button on the shirt was fastened, and she wasn't sure if he left it open because he liked it that way or because most of the buttons were missing.

Now there was only his face left. As she drew a step closer, she raised her head slightly and executed a quick study. Unlike his clothes, Tanner's face would never be described as comfortable. It was the strongest face she had ever seen. Like a desert mountain, his features were rugged and mysterious. Timeless.

"Okay," he said when she at last drew level with him, "this is where we stop and do the how-de-doos, maybe talk a little about the weather."

"How-de-do," she said obediently. "Weather, when used as a noun, could be described as the state of the atmosphere with regard to temperature, humidity—"

"Smart-ass," he said with an appreciative grin. "Now it's time for you to tell an amusing anecdote."

She frowned. "What if I don't know an amusing anecdote?"

"Make one up. It doesn't matter what you say, because this isn't about words. It's about hidden messages. I want you to pause at the funny part, laugh, and put a hand on his arm, like you're inviting him to share the joke. What you're really doing is inviting him to share a lot more. Because when you touch him, I want you to meet his eyes and give him The Look. Got it? Good. Now give it a try."

She wiped her free hand on her slacks and moistened her lips, gearing up. "Okay. Okay. Let's see. . . . Did I tell you about old Mr. Peterson and the time he—"

"Enough of the anecdote," he interrupted. "Get to the punch line. Touch, laugh . . . then let him have The Look."

She gave a short nod and cleared her throat. "He said it was the only way he could keep her from bothering him while he was working his crossword puzzles."

Forcing a laugh, she placed her hand on his upper arm and raised her eyes to his.

In her earlier examination Rae had instinctively avoided his eyes, and now she knew why. No one on earth had eyes like Tanner. Things were happening in those dark eyes. Spectacular events were taking place. Battles were being fought.

Look in Tanner's eyes, and you'll see the fires of hell raging.

She drew in a rough breath, reminding herself that looking into Drew's eyes wouldn't make her feel so uneasy.

At that moment Tanner made a short sound of contempt. "Jeez, Rae, is that the best you can do?

You look like you've been hit by a sudden attack of indigestion. There's supposed to be a message in your eyes. Something natural and basic. It should say, 'I'm a woman, you're a man, so what are you gonna do about it?' I know you can do this. I've seen The Look. Find it, turn it on, and you'll have your man wild with wanting you. One hint of it in your eyes, and he'll be fighting the urge to get down on his knees, right there on the street, and stick his tongue in your navel."

He dropped to his knees, threw his arms around her hips, and pressed his face to her stomach.

"You idiot." She slapped at the top of his head, squealing with laughter when she felt his teeth nibbling at her belly through her thin slacks. "Stop. That tickles . . . stop it!" But now she was laughing too hard to push him away. "Tanner . . ."

When he finally let go of her and rose to his feet, she gave him one last slap on the arm. "What are you trying to do?" she said, her voice uneven as she smoothed down her clothes. "I look like I've been in a dogfight."

He grinned. "I was trying to undo the zipper with my teeth. Another couple of seconds and I would have had it."

She shook her head. "Crazy man."

Moving to the bed, he flopped back across it, his hands folded beneath his head. "What's crazy about it? Making love through clothes is sexy as hell."

He raised his head and looked at her. "Remember when you and Johnny were in the backseat of his father's Buick? Or the times you ducked into the closet at a party so you could have a few minutes alone? Remember how exciting it was when you wanted to get as close as possible but circumstances wouldn't let you take your clothes off? You had to do the best you could through and around them."

Biting her lip, she stooped to pick up the magazine she had dropped when he grabbed her. "Actually . . ."

As the word faded away, he propped himself up on his elbows and studied her face, a look of disbelief growing on his. "You didn't jump into the backseat, did you? And you didn't sneak away at parties." Still staring at her, he slowly shook his head. "Unbelievable."

"Not that it's any of your business," she said, her voice stiff, "but Johnny and I made a conscious decision to wait until we were married to make love. We avoided heavy petting because it would have been too much of a temptation."

"Unbelievable," he repeated. "I didn't know people like you really existed. It's like something out of an old TV sitcom. I can see it now, you and Donna

Reed sitting at the kitchen table, the two of you drinking Bosco while you tell her how Johnny held your hand at the movies." He shook his head again. "Incredible."

Dropping back to the bed, he stared at the ceiling for a long time; then suddenly he was on his feet. "There's nothing else for it," he said with a careless shrug. "We'll have to go back and pick that up. Right now. It's an important part of your education."

The words were offhand, but something was different. Tanner wasn't playing the clown anymore. He was totally serious. He was going to reach back into the past and teach her about teenage petting.

With an effort she forced her head to move in two short, negative shakes. "No, really, Tanner. I—"

"What's the matter, sweetness?" He drew steadily closer. "Chicken? You want Drew, don't you?"

"That's not the point."

"Sure it is. That's why we're here. That's what all this is about."

"Maybe," she conceded, pushing the hair off her cheek in a distracted movement, "but I really don't think this is the way to—"

"You're not supposed to think, remember? You're supposed to feel."

He was moving behind her now, circling her, and she followed his movement with wary eyes.

"Tempting fate, teasing the senses, going right to the edge"—his voice was a lazy stroke across exposed nerve endings—"it's all a part of being hot."

She should probably leave now, she told herself. She should turn and run, and not slow down until there were at least a couple of miles between them. But something held her still. Something in those dark, unsettling eyes . . . or something in her.

"This is going to be a tactile sensation beyond silk." He was still moving, and the touch of his breath set up tingles on her ear and the back of her neck. "A necessary experience. Just think of this little exercise as a narrow mountain road. Every hairpin turn is going to bring you closer to your dream castle at the top."

The words whispered slowly across her face, and then he was behind her again, not quite touching but close enough for her to feel the heat from his body.

Drawing in a shaky breath, she closed her eyes, fighting desperately to resist the pull of his raspy voice. *Soft and rough. Water over gravel.*

"Let your imagination go, Rae. We're sixteen again, standing together in the shadows of your backyard. Your bedroom window is open, and the radio is playing. Hear it? Hear the words? All I need is the air I breathe . . . and you."

Sweet saints, she *heard* it. She heard the phantom beat throbbing through the air, and when his hands settled on her hips, applying a subtle but irresistible pressure, she found herself swaying with the music.

"That's right," he said, moving with her. "It's got you, hasn't it? The rhythm in the air . . . the rhythm inside both our bodies."

His hands slowly slid forward, his fingers spread out across her stomach. She didn't resist. She *couldn't* resist, not even when he pressed her hips back against his, their bodies still moving together with the inner beat.

"You want to make love." The husky words were inside her now, filling her up, mingling with the secret music and the warmth of his fingers. "But you can't. Not now. Any minute one of your parents could come out the back door and catch us. Feel your heart beating faster? There's danger here. But not enough to make you stop."

His head was bent, his lips next to her ear, so that she was a hairbreadth away from the rough excitement in his low laugh. "Oh no, you won't stop. Because you can't. You have to have one more touch, one more taste of the wildness."

Her eyelids raised lethargically when she felt

him move. He was in front of her now, and she stared up at him with dazed eyes as he held her hip to hip, their bodies still rocking from side to side, keeping time to the erotic beat.

"Maybe one of the neighbors is watching," he whispered, his eyes roaming restlessly over her face. "What will she think when she sees sweet little Rae letting her boyfriend put his hands on her body?"

His hands smoothed their way over her hips to explore the curves of her buttocks, then up her sides to the edge of her breasts, rubbing her through the cotton blouse.

"And what will she think when she sees sweet little Rae touching him back?" Keeping their lower bodies close, he brought her hands up to his chest. "You're desperate to feel bare skin under your fingers, and his shirt, just a thin layer of cotton, feels like armor plate because it's keeping you from what you need so badly."

He moved her hands, pushing them beneath his open shirt, letting them rest on the warm flesh. "That's right," he rasped against her forehead as her fingers, of their own accord, began to explore his muscled chest. "It hurts, doesn't it? Knowing that this is all you can have. Knowing that this one little taste of passion is all you'll get tonight. The thought of being caught is scary, but something is working inside you that's bigger than fear. More overpowering than fear. Something that's arousing you beyond your wildest dreams. And that's the knowledge that I . . . that your boyfriend wants to be inside you *so damned much*, it's driving him right out of his mind."

She swallowed a whimper as his fingers moved closer to the tips of her breasts. "You want the rest, you're crazy to feel it *all*, but you can't have it, not here, not now . . . and that makes the need more intense, more exquisite. The urgency is building in both of us, becoming intolerable. Things are happening to your body, changes are taking place. Feel them? Feel the blood surging to the sensitive places? Feel the warm, slick wetness? Every square inch of your body is alive with need, screaming out for release."

Her head had dropped back, her eyes closed, her head reeling as her breath came in short, shaky gasps.

Throbbing, throbbing, in her ears and her breasts, between her thighs. Rhythmic pulsation that kept time to the music. But there was no music. It was inside her. He had put it inside her. And now there was heat. She felt it through her clothes. It was the heat of his mouth, his breath . . . no, no, the heat of his words. Only words. But the words were touching her in secret places, moving her, gently rearranging her body so that she could feel the heat . . . so that she could feel it mingling with the throbbing need. He was . . . sweet heaven, he was—

She gave a moaning gasp, and her eyes flew open. Her breasts rose and fell in rapid, erratic movements as she backed awkwardly away from him.

He shifted his shoulders slightly. Had he moved? Had he always stood as he was standing now? He was watching her, just as she was watching him, but unlike her, he wasn't blinking in frantic confusion. He was simply watching. Watching and waiting, his dark eyes narrowed.

She could read nothing in his expression, nothing to tell her what had really happened. Had it only been words? Had she been shaken to the core by nothing more than an incredibly vivid description of an intimate act?

"Of course, it couldn't be an exact reproduction of the original," he said, as though he were picking up a conversation that had been momentarily interrupted, "but I think you get the idea."

His voice sounded normal. Or did it? she wondered, cutting uneasy eyes in his direction. She couldn't tell. She couldn't be sure. Normal was beyond her grasp. Every thought was out of focus, her senses haywire.

Raising his hand, he glanced at his watch. "You look tired. Why don't we call it quits for now and save the next lesson for another night?"

The next lesson? she thought, stifling a laugh of hysteria. She hadn't finished reeling from the current one. She didn't even want to think about what came next.

On the drive home she was still shaking inside, her hands clenched on the steering wheel in a death grip, her foot pressed to the floor in her urgency to outrun her thoughts, to outrun the knowledge that tonight she had crossed over an invisible line. She had unwittingly wandered into foreign territory.

Wild territory.

Tanner's territory.

Long after Rae had left, Tanner paced the small inner boundaries of his cabin, his movements filled with a restless urgency. Occasionally, without pausing, he raked an unsteady hand through his hair, ineffectively trying to shove the thoughts out of his head.

The hounds of hell were loose tonight. They were inside him, running mad, goading him, prodding him, demanding that he take action. A specific action. An action that required the presence of a woman who was probably sleeping soundly on a pile of lacy white pillows.

An instant later his harsh laugh broke through the silence. Sweet Jesus, he was paying now for his stupidity. Just a little blaze, he had told himself. He would get a little blaze going. Just for the hell of it. Just to show he could.

But from the very first it had gone wrong. He *knew* it. He knew it was going wrong, but he couldn't make himself stop. And so the little blaze had gotten out of control and was now inside him, burning him up.

Burning . . . him . . . up.

A growling groan of pain came from deep in his chest. Swiveling on his heels, he moved toward the door and took the three steps in one leap as he headed for the stable.

He would ride it out. He would take Loco, the wildest, meanest horse in this part of the country, and he would ride, hard and fast, across the open range.

He wouldn't stop until the demons were back in their cage and the fire in his gut had burned itself out.

Rae glanced at the digital clock beside the bed. Two A.M. The candy-striped nightshirt had been discarded hours ago, but tonight it didn't help. She was no closer to sleep than she had been at midnight.

Unbelievable, unthinkable memories filled the

room around her. Memories too vivid to be en-
dured. Every soft night sound, every touch of the
sheet, even the breeze stirred by the ceiling fan, all
reminded her of Tanner's lesson and her incredible
reaction. Even now, hours after the fact, every inch
of her body was aflame. He had left his imprint on
her, as surely as if he had used a branding iron.

With *words*.

Exhaling a soft groan, she sat up and covered
her face with her hands. Tonight, fully dressed and
sober as a judge, with a man she neither understood
nor trusted, Rae had almost—

But she didn't want to think about what had
almost happened. She didn't want to remember
the inward clinching of her body, the dawning of
exquisite pulsations at her center, sensations she
recognized instantly and had shut off before they
could take hold.

Brought on by *words*?

The most incredibly intimate act in nature. The
thorough giving over of self. Willingly, even joyful-
ly, allowing another human being to stand witness
to that moment of all-encompassing vulnerability.

With nothing more than words, Tanner had set
something loose inside her. But, dear sweet heaven,
she didn't want it set loose. Ever. She couldn't handle it. She wanted it to go back to its hiding place
and leave her alone.

Riding out a violent shudder, she slipped from the bed and walked to the window. The backyard, bathed in the platinum glow of moonlight, was a place of fantasy and peace.

Rae wanted to walk out there. She wanted to stand in the open air, her arms raised to the silver night. She wanted to feel the light summer breeze on her naked flesh, stroking her mouth, hardening the tips of her breasts, stirring the fine hair between her thighs.

And that impulse, that shocking urge, scared her almost as much as what had taken place in Tanner's cabin.

What was happening to her? Why, at this point in her life, was she discovering these incomprehensible, uncharacteristic cravings within herself? It didn't make sense.

Drawing in a deep, shaky breath, she spent the next ten minutes concentrating with fierce intensity on the flowers and shrubs, on the shadows thrown across the little rock terrace, but it was no use. The pattern of light and dark only reminded her of the night she first met Tanner. Fireworks and shadows. Lone Dees madness. The impact he had made on her with a single look from those dark devil's eyes.

In desperation she tried to conjure up a picture of Drew, the man she wanted to be the father of her children. The man who would never send her running into the night, afraid of her own feelings, doubting her emotional stability. Drew was steady. Solid as a rock. Totally secure.

And she couldn't even remember what color his eyes were.

Slumping down to the window seat, she bent over and hugged her bare legs to her chest. This had to stop. Somehow, she had to force reason into an unreasonable situation.

This feeling, the glorious madness she had felt when Tanner moved his body in time with hers and stroked her with husky words, wasn't all that extraordinary, she told herself. Every woman in town wanted him. Even the ones who condemned him in public saved their private moments for wondering what it would be like to have Tanner West in their beds.

Rae had seen the way women looked at him. Old and young, married and single, they all wanted him. Why should she be the exception? Lusting after Tanner was practically de rigueur.

Letting out a slow breath, she leaned back against the side of the window. This was good, she decided. Now she was getting somewhere.

Although she had always thought of herself as a supremely sensible person, she was still human. And the feelings Tanner brought out in her were probably some sort of echo of humankind's primitive past. Cavemen had short life spans. No time for dating, for exchanging phone numbers and astrological signs. It was a matter of see, want, have.

Tonight, some secret, primal urge in Rae had been ignited by a man who was himself primal, a walking call of the wild.

But it was a passing thing. She had to believe that. She couldn't make her attraction to Tanner more important than it was. Just because she had never experienced it before didn't mean it was anything out of the ordinary. Pure animal passion was something that happened all the time. She would have to accept it as a natural, albeit disconcerting, part of life.

And then she would simply have to learn to ignore it.

It was a sticky situation, but Rae was satisfied that she had found the solution. She had faced the facts, defined the problem, and mapped out a course of action.

So why wasn't she back in bed? Why was she still sitting in the window seat, rubbing her chin across up-drawn knees?

Because something was nagging at her, some difference—

That was it, she realized, sitting up straighter. She was different. In just a few short hours, she had changed. Something had been added to her mental and emotional makeup. Anticipation. Excitement. Acute awareness of possibilities. Passion for life.

For nine years she had been in a rut, plodding along, using routine to fill the empty spaces in her life, existing merely by rote. All the astonishing urges she had felt tonight meant she was coming out of her self-imposed shell. It meant she was finally opening herself up to life.

She gave a soft laugh as it dawned on her that Tanner, in his own infamous way, was doing exactly what he had told her he would do.

SIX

"I have a great idea." Rae held the phone between her chin and shoulder as she dug in her purse for her car keys.

"There are two kinds of people I instinctively distrust," Glenna said, her voice sounding even more sarcastic than usual through the telephone line. "The ones who say all it takes is a little willpower and the ones who tell me they have a great idea."

Grinning, Rae glanced over her shoulder to check her appearance in the hall mirror. Wide white hat, little white gloves, and a mint-green dress of handkerchief linen. Demure and discreet. Exactly right for a luncheon hosted by the Art and Historical Society or, as Glenna dubbed them, the Daughters

of Somebody Important Who's Dead Now So Why
Should I Care?

Rae had agreed to go to the luncheon weeks
ago, before she had taken steps to change her life.
Taken steps? She thought with an inward laugh.
What a tame way of putting it. Nothing that was
even remotely connected to Tanner could be called
tame. But for good or for bad, tomorrow night she
would go to his cabin for another lesson.

"Seriously, Glenna," she said, "why don't you
come out to the country club with us? I'm sure
Edna wouldn't mind."

"Edna might not mind, but I would. Any time
I want to eat creamed chicken and listen to snide
remarks about my weight and my single state, I can
go see my mother."

"But it's not just lunch. There's going to be a
lecture afterward. You could use some culture."

"Morris Lemson?" Glenna's tone was incredulous. "A man who has devoted his entire life
to string art? I need that like a yeast infection. If
I were you, I'd manage to break a leg in the next
few minutes. I can't believe you let Edna Live-
ly sucker you into this. She put on that poor,
pitiful-me act, and you bought it. That was really
dumb, Rae."

Rae leaned against the wall. "Edna's having a
tough time right now. Since her husband died—"

Glenna's short bark of laughter cut her off. "Since George died, Edna's been having the time of her life. Everyone keeps dropping by to check on her, bringing her food and little gifts, running errands for her, taking her places. That old lady's social life has improved about three hundred percent since she became a widow. Come on, Rae, admit it. She suckered you."

"If you want to call it that. I know Edna did some maneuvering, but I let her. I can't help thinking what it was like for me right after Johnny died. I was—" She broke off as the doorbell rang. "There she is. I hope you have a miserable day, you fink."

"I'm going to take a pumice stone to the calluses on my heels . . . and I'll still have a better time than you," Glenna said, laughing as Rae used an indelicate term and cut the connection.

Dicton's country club lay on the north edge of town. The main building, built of rock and glass, had a sleek, modern look to it. It was modern not because the community was modern, but because it had been built only twenty-five years earlier when the area's farmers, who did their socializing at the Masonic and VFW lodges, stopped being Dicton's most important citizens. The businesspeople who took over were more cosmopolitan. They understood about keeping up with the Joneses, and since Kliester had a country club, Dicton had to have one as well.

The club boasted two dining rooms. One was not much more than a snack bar where, in a bathing suit and bare feet, members could get a light lunch or something to drink. The other was elegant, quiet, and very formal. Ties and jackets were required for men, and no woman dared show up in slacks, no matter how dressy. It was in the latter room that the luncheon was being held.

The dining room was almost full when Rae and her neighbor arrived, and in every direction one cared to look there were people with the clean-cut, shiny look that wealthy Texans, even small-town Texans, always had.

Near the center of the room was L. D. Pryor—president of the town's largest bank—and his wife. Virg and Ruthie Embrey—Virg was an ex-linebacker who owned the town's only farm-equipment dealership—occupied a table near the podium. CeeCee Franklin sat at the table next to Virg and Ruthie. CeeCee's late grandfather made a fortune in the Kilgore oil fields, so the former whiled away her time spending the latter's money and collecting husbands. Today CeeCee was escorted by a young man who had the look of a Chippendale's dancer. Across the room, the minister of the First Baptist Church shared a table with an orthopedic surgeon and a prominent realtor. And, as Rae had expected, Drew was there with his glamorous houseguest.

After being seated at a table overlooking the terrace, Rae sipped iced tea and arranged her features in an expression of interest while her neighbor talked, quietly and unremittingly, about the joys and sorrows of backyard gardening.

Rae liked Edna, but after a sympathetic nod and a couple of "Oh dears", what else could be said in response to a treatise on the little white bugs that eat begonias? Using pumice on heel callus was beginning to look better and better.

Just when Rae reached the point of wondering what would happen if she fell asleep over the herb-and-tomato appetizer, Edna made a choking sound and went totally still, her stunned attention fixed on a point beyond Rae.

At almost the same moment Rae became aware of the low murmur of shock that was spreading rapidly across the room. Turning in her seat, she looked around the room, searching for the source. Her puzzled gaze slid past the entrance then returned in a neck-snapping double-take.

Tanner stood just inside the entrance, lazily surveying the dining room.

His strong, tanned features were composed, as though elegant little luncheons were his normal Saturday fare, but the laughing devil in his eyes was having a field day.

In honor of the occasion he wore a toast-brown

jacket and a dress shirt the color of ripe wheat, not so different from others in the room. That, however, was where the resemblance ended. The required tie was draped around the open collar of his shirt, and the shirt was tucked neatly into faded skintight jeans.

A desperado with a sense of humor, she thought, letting her gaze linger on the worn, scuffed boots that completed his ensemble. Dicton's bad boy, bent on causing a stir. Carelessly, casually rebellious.

And sexy enough to make every woman in the room feel a little zing in her nether regions.

Edna, obviously feeling the zing, fidgeted in her seat. "Well, I never. That can't be Tanner West. Why is he here?" She reached across the table to tug urgently at Rae's sleeve. "You don't suppose he has his horse outside? Oh dear, what if he— You know, he doesn't quite look civilized, does he, even with—Did he cut his hair?"

"No," said Rae, her voice unsteady. "No, it looks like it's tied back with a little strip of leather."

A gasp came from Edna. Then, again, weakly: "Well, I never."

Rae had to swallow several times and stare determinedly at her hands until the urge to laugh subsided. The rest of the room seemed to be holding its breath, all eyes turned toward the man who was now being shown to a table.

Something strange always happened whenever Tanner walked into sight. Rae had noticed it before. It wasn't only that people reacted with automatic, electrified interest. It was something in the air, as though the molecules of nitrogen and oxygen suddenly went berserk, caroming off each other in excitement, jolted out of their natural order by his presence.

As lunch continued, Rae listened to the buzz of scandalized whispers and nervous titters that gradually smoothed out until, by the time dessert was served, people were again talking in normal voices.

Normal luncheon voices but by no means a normal luncheon topic, was Rae's guess. And although she couldn't hear their words, she was very much afraid that poor Mr. Lemson was not going to have the undivided attention of his audience.

" . . . and next I'd like to present a reproduction of a sixth-century icon. Note the way I've used gilded string to . . ."

Lunch was over, and the company's sporadic regard was turned toward Morris Lemson, a small, nondescript man who was taking them, block by block, on a tour of St. Petersburg, describing in minute detail the Byzantine art that he had been moved to translate into string.

Stifling a yawn, Rae let her attention wander. Eventually, inevitably, her gaze came to rest on Tanner. He sat with his chair tipped back against the wall, one knee propped against the table. For a moment she thought he was asleep, then she saw that his attention was held by something below table level. His hands were moving, but she couldn't see what he was doing because her view was blocked by a stout woman sitting at the table next to him.

Her curiosity well and truly piqued, Rae twisted slightly in her chair, craning her neck to see. What was he doing?

At that moment Tanner looked up and caught her watching him. With an audacious wink he raised his hands to chest level. Strong, tanned hands. Hands that were interwoven with twine. A Jacob's ladder.

While Morris talked, Tanner had been creating his own string art.

Rae's lips began to twitch, and she glanced quickly away from him, drawing in several deep breaths to keep the bubble of laughter from surfacing.

Impossible, intractable man, she thought, taking care not to look in his direction again.

When the lecture finally ended, the company moved en masse to the terrace for coffee and almost immediately broke up into small clusters. Clusters that excluded. They stood around the pool in tightly braided groups and talked in low voices, gossiping about the people in the next group, or more likely, gossiping about the tall, lean man who stood alone at the opposite end of the pool.

Since Edna had quickly spotted two fellow gardeners, Rae was free to make her way to the serving table alone, and as she was passing the mayor and his wife, one of those unaccountable lulls that visits every gathering fell across the terrace.

In the hush the tail end of a sentence was heard, sounding unnaturally loud in the surrounding silence.

" . . . guarantee you, it would take a lot more money than Old Joe has to make Tanner acceptable to the decent people in this town."

Rae caught her breath in a gasp of shock and, along with most of the people around her, turned her gaze toward Virg Embrey, the man who had spoken.

When he saw that he was the center of attention, Virg flushed and raised his chin. "I don't care," he said as his wife tried to shush him. "Everyone knows it's the truth. There are some people you shouldn't have to socialize with. That's why we have a country club. It's not right for Joe McCallister to let his thieving bastard son use his membership to come out here and—"

The ex-football star broke off abruptly, his eyes

widening as the color drained from his large, square face.

The subject of Virg's tirade had moved around the end of the pool and was calmly making his way toward the small knot of people.

When he reached them, Tanner looked down at Ruthie Embrey and smiled. "Ma'am," he said, politely greeting the petite blonde.

Then with a casual, almost elegant movement, he turned and tossed her husband into the swimming pool.

Rae's triumphant "Yes!" was drowned out in the uproar that followed. Several of Virg's astonished friends were stooping to help the big man out of the water, while the rest of the crowed gathered around to offer vehement words of sympathy and condemnation. But even the ones who were the most forthcoming with their sympathy and the most outspoken in their condemnation had an avid gleam of excitement in their eyes.

Drew, standing with Lynda near the serving table, turned, and for a moment his eyes met Rae's. As though they shared a secret joke, he moved his right hand in a quick thumbs-up gesture, then with a soft laugh he moved to join the crowd by the pool.

As Rae was watching Drew try to mollify Virg—dripping wet and full of blustering fury—she again caught sight of Tanner.

As before, he stood separate from the others. But now he was watching Rae. And although his dark eyes were ablaze with the wild, demonic light, other things were at work. Emotions her heart recognized. The same way she had recognized them on the night of the Lone Dees dance.

Before she could stop herself, Rae took an awkward, involuntary step toward him. But something he saw in her face, something in her expression, caused his features to harden, and with a short, almost soundless laugh, he turned to the crowd and bowed.

And then, without a backward look, he walked away.

That night Virg Embrey's impromptu baptism was the main topic of conversation in Dicton. To the Burger Barn, the Stop-N-Shop, and front porches all across town, the word spread.

By Sunday morning the story could be heard in a dozen different versions, the most popular of which was that Tanner had gotten drunk and started flinging people—without regard to sex, race, or creed—into the swimming pool.

It was the never-ending gossip that had Rae heading out of town Sunday afternoon. Driving with no destination in mind, she wound up on

Highway 101, gratefully mingling her Volvo with cars that didn't belong to Dicton and whose occupants had no idea who she was, nor did they care. The small taste of anonymity was refreshing.

Fifteen miles west of town, she came to a little roadside park, a small paved loop off the highway with a couple of cement picnic tables and a trash can set in the shade of a cluster of ancient cedar trees. Parked next to one of the tables was a mud-splashed, battered green pickup. Tanner's truck.

Afterward, she couldn't figure out why she did it. She wasn't an impulsive person, and it certainly wasn't something she had thought out. But for whatever reason, a minute later she found herself parking her car behind the green pickup.

Tanner, sitting on top of one of the picnic tables, was feeding scraps of his lunch to some sparrows, and only when she stepped from her car and moved toward the table did he tip back his hat and acknowledge her presence.

"If I didn't know better"—the words were low and lazy—"I'd say you were chasing me. What's the matter, sweetness, couldn't you wait for tonight? Need a little Tanner fix?"

Her jaw tightened, and she almost turned and walked away. The only the thing that stopped her was the knowledge that she would be doing exactly what he expected her to do. She could see him watching her, waiting for her reaction, almost willing her to turn tail and run.

Drawing in a slow breath, she smiled at him. "Hello, Tanner. Nice day, isn't it?"

With a short bark of laughter, he took off his hat and used it to dust off a place for her near his feet. "Take a load off. Don't worry, I won't bite . . . not unless you ask real nice."

Ignoring the taunt, she sat down and glanced up at him. "Is this how you spend your day off?" she asked, gesturing toward the birds.

"I'm a multifaceted man." He scattered some more bread. "This is my Saint Francis side. If you'd stopped a couple of minutes earlier, you would've seen Bambi and Thumper frolicking at my knee."

"Which side did we see yesterday?"

He chuckled. "I'd give a nickel for a picture of the look on Virg's face when he hit the water. I didn't know y'all had so much fun out at the country club."

"Why did you go?" she asked, genuinely interested.

After tossing the last of the bread toward the birds, he crumpled his lunch sack into a ball. "I was falling down on the job. It was time I shook things up a little, gave 'em all something to talk about." His lips spread in a wicked grin. "I bet they're going at it this morning. I wonder how many sermons I inspired."

She laughed, recalling the reason she had driven out of town. "They may be talking, but it's the general consensus that if ever anyone deserved dunking, it's Virg Embrey. He was unforgivably rude."

"That's not why I did it," he said, shooting a look in her direction. "Do you think that's the first time I've ever heard that kind of talk? I did it because everyone was waiting for it. Not that particular thing, but something. You saw them. They were all watching me, wondering when I'd do something outrageous. It was practically my civic duty."

She had been studying his face as he spoke; now she said, "You're a strange man."

"Not so strange." He swatted at a fly buzzing between them. " 'If you prick me, do I not bleed?' And then do I not break your face? A long time ago the people in Dicton labeled me an outlaw. I'm 'that wild Tanner West,' the guy who fights anything that moves and screws anything that stands still." He moved his shoulders in a careless shrug. "Back when Hardy's gas station got robbed, nobody bothered to ask what I was doing that night. Since two of the guys I hung around with were involved, everybody just took it for granted that I was too. Ask any one of them about the last time he saw me drunk, and he'll tell you it was only last week. The truth is, I haven't had more than a couple of drinks at one sitting in over six years."

"And that doesn't bother you?"

"Why should it bother me? People have to have order in their lives. They have to. So what they do is make their own reality. Truth for them is whatever's easiest to swallow."

His voice was casual, almost disinterested, but she thought his eyes were the most cynical she had ever seen.

"It's not my job to change them," he went on. "I'm the bad guy. Anything else would cut up their peace. It would make them uncomfortable if they thought I had the same hopes and dreams as every man."

He glanced at her. "What's that look for? You don't think I dream? Keeping Dicton stirred up is only a sideline. My main work is dreaming."

He turned and lay back on the table, his hat on his chest, one knee bent as he stared up at the rough canopy of green. "I've got some land out in West Texas, land I've been paying on for more than ten years now. Every spare penny I can get my hands on goes to that land. It's not even a thousand acres, but it's mine."

He smiled. "That land, that's the canvas my dream is painted on. There's just a little trailer out there now, but someday I'll build a house up on this little rise I found. Out in West Texas, a little rise is like a mountain, and from the top you can see clear into tomorrow if you look hard enough. There are a few trees on it, enough to give some relief from the sun, so that's where I'll put my house. Right in the middle of those trees. It'll be a real family place with a big porch running all the way around it, and grass and flowers in the yard."

He sat up again. "And I want children, Rae. A whole damn houseful of kids."

The enthusiasm in his voice made her blink in astonishment. This was a side of him she had never seen, had never expected expect to see, a side she would never have believed possible.

"There's a little river running along the back edge of my land where I can take my kids fishing. And I'm going to teach them to ride and how to make things grow." He glanced at her. "And they'll all have a sense of humor. I'll tell them about the really important things in life, and teach them how to laugh at all the rest."

Frowning, he said, "I don't carry any excess baggage around with me. My horse, my truck, and the shirt on my back, that's about it. So the mother of my kids will have to bring all that stuff with her. Family pictures for the walls, the quilt her granny made, the ugly vase that Great-uncle Eli gave to Great-aunt Sadie on their fiftieth anniversary, the family Bible with all the names written in it. Things like that give kids a feeling of security."

He fell silent, his expression distant, as though he were actually seeing the spreading panorama of his dream. When he spoke again, his voice was lower, huskier. "And there'll be two rocking chairs out on the front porch, so that in the evening when it's cool, I can sit beside the woman I love and watch our children play."

Sliding off the other side of the table, he moved a couple of steps away, his back to her. "She'll be a special kind of woman. A woman who'll stick by me, even in bad times. But not grudgingly. She'll stay because of all the places in the world, this is where she wants to be. She'll be a woman who knows what forever means. A woman who—"

Although she couldn't see his face, she heard the change in his voice and saw the sudden tension in his shoulders. "I can almost hear what you're thinking," he said harshly. "You're thinking, Tanner West with a woman like that?" He gave a short, rough laugh. "Well, you're right. Hell, I'm not stupid. I know it's just a dream. But any man can dream. You see what I'm saying? Any man, no matter who he is, no matter what he is, can have a dream. Can't he?"

He turned around and took a step toward her. *"Can't he?"*

The question was filled with urgency and a

strange kind of helpless anger. And when she looked deep into his eyes, she saw the same thing she had seen the day before. Vulnerability. Desperate, aching need.

"Yes," she said, in a hoarse whisper, "any man can dream."

And so could any woman.

Hearing his dream, so close to her own, brought a throbbing ache to her chest and the sting of tears to her eyes. And for one brief moment, she had the crazy urge to go to this man, her self-appointed tormentor, and gather him into her arms, to give comfort and draw it from him.

A shout of harsh laughter shattered her thoughts. Blinking in confusion, she raised her head to look at him.

He was watching her, those dark devil's eyes narrowed and intense. "And if you'll buy that, I have a bridge I'd like to tell you about," he said with a malicious smile twisting his lips. "I really had you going for a minute, didn't I?"

He shook his head with contempt and turned to move toward his truck. "Now you see why I tease you," he threw back at her. "You're so damned gullible."

When he reached the front of his truck, he paused and, without looking back, said, "You coming out to the cabin tonight?"

"Yes. . . . yes, I'll be there."

Although he had definitely intended her to be, Rae wasn't angry. She wasn't angry because she didn't believe a word of his final taunt. She might be gullible, but she knew that his dream had been no lie. It was real.

And that was why he had been so emphatic in his denial. When Tanner realized that he had given her a piece of himself, he had tried to grab it back before she had a chance to look at it.

It had taken two years, but Rae finally understood. Now she knew why, of all the people he knew, Tanner had chosen her to antagonize, to tease and torment. He chose her because sometimes when Rae looked at him, she saw who he really was.

He hated her for that, for seeing and understanding, for knowing things about him that no one else knew.

He said the town had labeled him an outlaw, but he was wrong. Tanner himself had done the labeling. It was his defense, his way of getting in the first punch.

No one could hurt Tanner, she thought as she walked slowly back to her car, because he pushed everyone away before they got close enough to do any damage.

SEVEN

On Thursday afternoon when Rae passed through the outer office, the room was empty. Glenna was home nursing a summer cold, which meant no one was there to ask why Rae had stayed so long at the courthouse, and no one was there to notice that she had a most peculiar look in her eyes.

Four days had gone by since Rae had met Tanner at the roadside park, and during those days she had gone to his cabin twice. As though they had reached an unspoken agreement, neither mentioned the accidental meeting. The lessons simply went on as before. Tanner continued to bark out orders, and Rae continued to be torn between laughter and frustration in his presence.

And even while Rae acknowledged her newfound openness to life—the same openness that made it necessary for her to constantly fight against the sensual pull of this complex man—there were times that Rae wondered if she would ever be the woman he was trying to turn her into.

But today, in the span of a few short minutes, everything had changed.

When she walked into her own office, she shut the door and leaned back against it. A moment later she gave her head a bemused little shake and laughed aloud.

"Gonna let me in on the joke?"

The high-backed chair behind her desk swung around. Tanner was slouched down in the chair, his dark eyes fixed on her with interest.

"You look like you just won the lottery," he said. "Or a big case. Don't tell me the electric company is going to settle with Seraphina Rodale."

Rae pushed away from the door and crossed the room. Placing both hands flat on the desk, she leaned toward him. "Right here," she said slowly, "right here in front of me, wearing dusty boots, indecent jeans, and . . . do you *own* a shirt that doesn't have half the buttons missing? Right here, sits a genius."

She drew in a calming breath and kept her eyes level with his. "There have been times in the past two years when I've wanted to strangle you. And there have been times that I've wished you to perdition.

But know this about me: I am no shirker of facts. Rae Anderson does not dodge the truth. And this is the inescapable, unvarnished truth. You, Tanner West, desperado par excellence, Dicton's most celebrated bad boy, are a true genius. If I were wearing a hat, I would take it off to you. Since I'm not, I'll do the next-best thing." She extended her right hand across the desk. "I'll shake the hand of the man who worked a miracle."

After eyeing her hand for a moment, he raised his dark gaze to her face. "Is Petey DuPuy back in town?"

Swinging away from the desk, she threw back her head and laughed. "I'm not drunk, at least not the way you think."

With an abrupt movement she straightened her features and glanced back over her shoulder, giving him an intentionally provocative look. "Don't you know? Can't you tell? You're an astute man, Tanner. And you probably know more about women than all the other men in this county put together."

She moved around the desk and stood slightly behind him, bending down to let her lips brush across his ear. "Put all your senses to work on the problem, sweetness," she said in a husky whisper. "Go with your instincts. Listen to your inner substance. What's it saying to you, Tanner?"

He grabbed her hands and pulled her around so

he could see her face. "It's telling me your gears are sticking."

She laughed again and slipped out of his grasp. On the other side of the desk she turned to face him. "Wrong. I'll tell you what it's saying. It's saying this woman"—she jabbed her chest with one finger—"is hot. Not mild. Not sunny. Not balmy or temperate or clement. Not even normal for this time of the year with a warm front moving in. This woman is capital H-O-T, *hot*."

She licked her thumb and applied it to her hip with a hissing sound. "Sizzling," she said, giving the word three slow syllables, her lips pouting.

Tanner's head was drawn back, his eyes narrowed as he watched her. "I don't know," he muttered, "I might have to vote for balmy. What's going on?"

She shook her head in reproach. "Modesty doesn't become you. Don't you get it? It *worked*. You said you would show me how to attract a man, and that is just exactly what you did."

She dropped down in the chair opposite him, trying to catch her breath. "I ran into Drew a little while ago and—This is where I pause for effect." She paused for effect. "I ran into Drew at the courthouse, and we started talking . . . I didn't even have to do the laugh-touch-look thing. We just started talking, and, I don't know, I could tell he was looking at me in a completely different way. I can't describe it, but it was different." A soft laugh of disbelief escaped her. "And we have a date for tomorrow night. Dinner and dancing."

Pulling herself up straighter, she shot a look at him. "You'll be interested in this part. I asked him about Lynda, and he said she flew to New York this morning, but he assumed she'd be back because she left all her things at the ranch. He *assumed* . . . as though he didn't much care one way or the other. He really seems to—"

She broke off, suddenly aware of Tanner's reaction, or rather, his lack of reaction. "Why are you so quiet? Why aren't you celebrating with me? Let's hear some huzzahs and hip-hip-hoorays. When Lynda comes back, you can step in, just the way we planned. The unholy alliance worked. We did it."

He rubbed his chin, his gaze turned away from her, his expression thoughtful. "I don't know."

"What do you mean you don't know?" she asked with growing belligerence. "Drew asked me out. He *noticed* me, Tanner."

"Not bad," he allowed with a nod. "At least, it's not bad for a start, but what happens if you go out tomorrow night and suddenly turn into Miss Wholesome? It's not like we've wiped out all traces of her, you know. I can still hear echoes of 'Look at me, I'm Sandra Dee' when you forget yourself."

"But—"

"Look, I'm not trying to take anything away from you. You've made a hell of a lot of progress. If Drew is looking at you in a different way, it's because he sees a different woman. The changes are subtle, so you may not have noticed them, but they're definitely there. In the way you move, the way you hold yourself, the way you've opened yourself up to the world around you."

He gave a nod in her direction. "Look at what you're doing right now. You're moving your fingers on the arms of the chair, feeling the texture. And you weren't even aware of it. Your senses are on the alert all the time now." He let his gaze drift over her body. "Of course, wearing all that silk next to your skin hasn't hurt anything."

She felt her face flood with heat as she became intensely conscious of the red silk bra and panties.

He gave a low chuckle. "Don't look at me like that. I didn't peek through your window, and I didn't ask Paula. I can just tell. The point is, it's not enough. Everything we've done so far was to get his attention. Now we have to work on keeping it."

He stood up and moved from behind the desk. "Trust me on this one, Rae. We're not through yet. Come out to the cabin tonight, and we'll do a little rehearsal dinner."

She turned her head, following his progress to the door. "You're cooking?"

"I can cook. I can do anything I want when I put my mind to it." Then, just before he walked out, he added, "It's a good thing to remember about me."

Tanner had covered his small kitchen table with a white tablecloth, and a single candle was the only illumination in the room. Because, he told her, that's the kind of snotty little place Drew would take her to.

Sitting at the table, she watched while he occupied himself with something on the stove. "How can you see what you're doing?" When he didn't answer, she shifted restlessly in her chair. "I really don't understand why this is necessary. I know how to keep up my end of a dinner conversation, and I don't think Drew's going to be disgusted with my table manners."

"This isn't about social chitchat and etiquette. It's about maintaining a sexual attraction while you're doing ordinary things. Just because you've got him interested doesn't mean you can relax and be yourself."

Frowning, she rested her chin in the palm of one hand. "Will I ever be able to do that? Be myself, I mean."

He glanced over his shoulder at her. "Sure. But we're not through with the two-by-four yet. You have to use sex appeal to get him to stay long enough to want to know the real you."

When he moved closer to put a plate in front of her, she looked up at him. "I know this was my idea, but sometimes it feels dishonest. Like I'm setting traps."

"It's not dishonest. In fact, there's nothing more honest. Watch the birds sometimes, check out the rituals they go through at mating time." He sat in the chair opposite her. "We're talking about nature, sweetness."

"Yes, I guess so," she said, still doubtful. "But— Wait a minute, I recognize this." She glanced from her plate to his face, her tone accusing. "You didn't cook. You got this from Joe Baker's Little Italy. It's the only place in America that serves pasta with a jalapeño garnish."

"I said I can cook. I didn't say I was going to." He reached across the table and filled her glass from a bottle of red wine. "Okay, here's the program. We're going to get a sexy little conversation going while we eat. This is going to be tough because of the way your brain works. All that honest, forthright stuff keeps dragging you down. But tomorrow night I want you to point your mind in a different direction. I want you to twist the meaning of everything he says, turn it into something provocative. Double entendre the poor sucker into submission. If he says the dinner rolls are hard, you give him a look and tell him hard is your favorite thing."

He grinned at her reaction. "Stop gagging. It's just another whack from the two-by-four."

Although Joe's lasagna was, as always, excellent, and Tanner did his best to set the mood, Rae couldn't take the practice conversation seriously, and more often than not, her replies sent them both into whoops of laughter.

After one particularly outrageous innuendo, he covered his face with one hand and groaned. "You're hopeless, absolutely hopeless." Pushing his chair away from the table, he stood up. "Okay, enough of the snotty little restaurant, now it's time for some boot scootin'." "Boot scooting" was the local term for dancing. "Come on, Rae, get your little ass in gear."

"In gear for what? I don't need you to teach me how to dance, if that's what you're talking about. I can dance."

"No, you can't."

Her chin came up; her look was belligerent. "I *can* dance. I took lessons for six years. And then Johnny and I used to—"

"What?" he prompted. "Go to those schmoozy little clubs in Fort Worth and let your feet go mellow? This is Dicton, and there are a total of two places here to dance. You could go to the club at the Overnight Inn where a couple of jokers with hair down to their butts abuse electric guitars for the entertainment of a bunch of teenagers who are more interested in going to the bathroom to buy pills from some kid who emptied out his mother's medicine cabinet, or you can go to J. T.'s out on Highway 101 for some country dancing. Do you know anything about country dancing?"

She drew in a slow, irritable breath. "You know I don't."

"Right." He stooped to turn on the radio, twisting the dial until he found what he was looking for. "We'll keep it slow until you learn the steps. Watch me. Step, step, slide. Step, step, slide. Got it? Okay, let's go."

Reaching out, he pushed one hand under her hair, cradling her neck firmly in his warm palm as he clasped her right hand in his left.

"Is Drew going to grab me by the neck?" she asked, acutely aware of the way his thumb was moving against the sensitive flesh behind her ear.

"Probably not, but this is the way I do it. It doesn't matter. The steps are the same. Put your hand on my hip."

Bossy bastard, she fumed silently. Raising her hand, she let it rest lightly on his waist.

With a short sound of exasperation, he took the hand and planted it firmly on his hip. "My hip, Rae, my hip. For Pete's sake, loosen up a little, you're not going to touch anything exciting right there."

Oh yeah? she thought as they began to move. Try telling that to my hand.

"You're not putting enough into it. When you step back, throw your shoulder in that direction." He shifted his hands to her shoulders and showed her how to move as they danced. "That's better. If you're gonna live in Dicton, you're gonna have to dance Dicton."

Reclaiming her neck, he swung her around, and they began to move in the opposite direction. "Out here, when we dance, we dance. It's not elegant, but by God, it's alive. Everything we have and are is in this music. Don't just listen to it, swallow it, inhale it. Hear that guitar trill? Move your hips with it. Can't you feel it bouncing around inside you?"

The fact that Tanner was a wonderful dancer shouldn't have surprised her and wouldn't have if she had once let herself think about the natural grace in his walk. Before she knew what was happening, she was caught up in the energetic, enthusiastic movements.

"Why do you hold my hand so high?"

"This." He let go of her neck and twirled her under his arm. "Twirling is also the cause of one of the biggest setbacks in the women's movement. No, really," he added, catching her skeptical glance. "You see women at the head of big corporations, you see them laying bricks, you even see them in the boxing ring. But when's the last time you saw one leading out on the dance floor? That's because most women are shorter than their dancing partner. She couldn't twirl him."

He paused, his dark devil's eyes sparkling. "The women's movement did all right by sex though. It improved the whole process of making love. Women can take the lead in the bedroom and—"

"I do not wish to discuss what the women's movement did for sex," she said, her voice repressive.

Although the unholy glitter lingered in his eyes, he let it go with nothing more than a laugh.

It was after trying to keep up with "Dumas Walker" that Rae finally had to take a break. When they returned to the table, she was out of breath and laughing from pure enjoyment.

"Okay, I admit it," she said. "You were right. I needed the dance lesson. Now where are we?"

"Still at J. T.'s. We're having a drink to cool off." He refilled her wineglass, then, leaning forward, met her eyes across the table. "Okay, pick up your glass, take a sip, and lick the wine off your lips while you're staring into my eyes."

"Oh please," she muttered under her breath. "I will not be able to do this. Not if my life depends on it. It's stupid and juvenile and corny, and no intelligent man would fall for it anyway."

"Shut up and do it," he ordered.

Rolling her eyes, she lifted her glass and took a sip, then ran her tongue over her upper lip. Raising her eyes to his, she saw that all his attention was now focused on her mouth. As they sat staring at each other, Rae could feel the heat rise in her face, but even more intense was the heat that settled in her lips where his glittering gaze stroked her.

"I wish you could see your eyes right now," he murmured. "Who'd have thought baby blue could ever look like that?"

Glancing away, she cleared her throat noisily. "Did I do it right?" The breathless tremor in her voice was barely noticeable. "I have never understood what this lip-licking thing is supposed to accomplish."

"You're such a whine-baby," he said with a low chuckle. "The lip-licking thing, which you've just demonstrated so effectively, will have him wondering what it would feel like to have that little pink tongue flicking across any and all of his naked body parts."

She choked. She coughed. Her heart jumped, and her hand shook. Then, in what somehow seemed an inevitable outcome, she spilled the wine.

For a long moment Rae simply stared down at the stain that was spreading across the front of her dress. Then she slowly raised her head. "Stop laughing. Tanner, I mean it. Tanner, dammit, stop laughing!"

"Good move, Rae," he said, his voice unsteady, his tone admiring. "I'd go for it in a minute. I really would. Woman marinated in red wine is one of my favorite things. But you might think twice about trying it on Drew."

"Just shut up. It wouldn't have happened if I had been with Drew. He doesn't say things that get me flustered." She pulled the dress away from her breasts. "This is going to be a sticky mess when it starts to dry."

"No problem," he said, standing up. "Take it off, and I'll throw it in the washing machine."

"You have a washing machine?"

"What'd you think, I take all my stuff out and beat it on a rock?"

Rising to her feet, she followed him across the room. "If I had thought about it at all, which I guarantee you I have *not*, because I have better things to do than think about how you manage your household chores, I would have assumed that one of your women—"

He gave her a look that cut her off. "My women," he said with wicked gleam in his eyes, "are definitely not for laundry. Here, you can wear this while your things are washing."

She had followed him into a small room that appeared to be a combination clothes closet and utility room, and now he was handing her a short burgundy silk robe with lapels and wrap belt of midnight blue.

Rae recognized the soft tie belt. He had used it to teach her how to respond to the call of her senses.

"It was a gift," he explained when she stared down at the robe with one brow raised. "She didn't hang around long enough to get to know me, to find out I'm not the type to wear robes. The only time I ever put it on, I felt like a Noël Coward mutant."

The explanation was made in an offhand way, but the cynicism was back in his eyes, and, as always, it brought a sharp pang of compassion. No, not compassion, she amended silently, regret. She deeply regretted that Tanner had ever had to discover the things in life that now made him so bitter.

In the bathroom she stripped off her clothes, handed them to him through a carefully cracked door, then glanced around the room. The wine was already getting uncomfortably tacky. What she needed was a quick shower.

Although Tanner's bathroom was as impersonal as the rest of his house, it was a nice little room. Sage-green ceramic tile on the floor and halfway up the wall. White pedestal sink and matching toilet. Brightly lit mirror over the sink.

But nowhere, not in any direction, was there either a shower or a tub.

She moved back to the door. "Tanner? Tanner, where's the bathtub?"

"I don't have a bathtub," he yelled. "You'll have to use the shower."

She looked around again. "I hate to be the one to give you the bad news, but your shower's been stolen."

His laughter reached her clearly. "Open the door directly opposite you."

She had seen the door he was referring to but had assumed it was a linen closet. A second later, when she opened it, a warm breeze brushed across her face. Redwood floor. Canvas sides. Looking up, she saw stars.

"It's outside," she murmured; then, glancing over her shoulder, she raised her voice: "Tanner, your shower is outside."

"Don't be so ordinary," he called back. "You'll like it."

Muttering under her breath, she stepped onto the miniature redwood deck, closed the door behind her, and raised wary eyes to the outsized shower head. Industrial strength, the kind used on factory workers who have been exposed to radioactive material.

It figured. Everything about Tanner was emphatic. More. Bigger. Bolder. A rebellious departure from the customary.

With a grimace of anticipation, she turned on the water and stepped under it, then immediately sucked in a sharp breath as the water hit her bare flesh with stinging force.

It was amazing, she thought minutes later. Not only was she getting used to it, she was enjoying it. The miniature Niagara Falls, the cool of the night air, the stars shining overhead. Who would have thought a shower could be so exciting?

"Nice, isn't it?"

Rae must have jumped a foot, her gaze darting around in panic. "Where are you?"

"Right beside you."

Swinging around, she turned her back on the voice and crossed her arms on her breasts, grabbing her shoulders with both hands. "Go away."

He chuckled. "You're covering up, aren't you? You idiot, I can't see you. No X-ray vision ... it's the only way you can tell me and Superman apart."

"I don't care," she muttered. Even if he couldn't

see through the canvas, his presence was making her damned uncomfortable. "Go away."

"Forget about me. And forget all your silly little hang-ups. Look up, Rae. Is that the most spectacular thing you've ever seen in your life? All the way down through history, people have been looking up at that sky, fascinated by the sheer immensity of it."

His lazy voice reached out to her, gentling her, easing away the tension. "Just think of it. That sky has seen it all, the whole pitiful history of man. It was there when mankind took its first baby steps, back when people were natural and free, back before society went into its rule-making frenzy."

Rae found herself caught and held by the smoky voice, intrigued against her will by his story. Somehow, without being aware of having moved, she was out of the water, leaning against the side of the shower, her body turned slightly so that her right side pressed against the canvas.

"The way you are now, naked under the stars, is the most natural thing in the world. Clothes, houses, college degrees, eating with the right fork . . . all those things are walls we use to keep us separate from nature. Over there is wildness and disorder. On this side, civilization. Separate and therefore better. But the wall is artificial, an arrogance on the part of man. We could build the Great Wall of

China around us, and it wouldn't change anything, thank God. It doesn't get any better than nature, and the two of us, we're a part of it. When you get down to basics, the same stuff that's in a giraffe, a bluebird, and a honey bee is also in us."

The words weren't new. It was a simple theme that she had heard before. But this time something was different. He made all the complicated notions laid on by the makers of rules seem frivolous. He was telling her to take pride in her kinship with all the other creatures living on the earth. He was telling her that the majesty of nature was in her.

"And just like the giraffe, bluebird, and honey bee, we have, built in us all, the overpowering need to merge with the opposite sex." His voice was deeper now, and filled with a sensuality that came to her in velvety strokes. "We do our merging behind closed doors and between perfumed sheets, and we fool ourselves into thinking it's a civilized act. But take away the doors and sheets, put it out on a hill, under this unending sky, and you see it for what it really is. Primitive. Uninhibited. Bold and free. Totally, unapologetically natural."

This was what he had tried to tell her weeks ago in her office, that she had she spent her whole life building walls between herself and her true nature. Was he right? Did she have that kind of glorious wildness in her?

"Remember, the sky has seen it all." He was leaning on the canvas now. Because she was a step above him, his shoulder was level with hers, and she could feel the weight of him pressing against her. "For time out of mind, it's seen those two shapes, lying together in the cool grass on a hilltop with starlight giving their skin a silver sheen that can't be copied by any man-made lamp."

His voice was getting to her. It was really, really getting to her. Erotic, like being rubbed by raw, nubby silk. Enticing, provoking, seducing—

"One he, one she, the way it was meant to be. The sky isn't shocked to see her legs wrapped around him. And it isn't offended by the things he's doing to her. It knows that this particular she is enjoying what this particular he can give her, welcoming it, opening herself up for more. Without restraint, without apology. No touch forbidden, no act unthinkable. Whatever feels good is right."

There was a long, incredibly tense pause, and then he whispered, "Can you see it, Rae?"

"Yes," she said, her voice low and hoarse. "Yes, I can see—"

At that very moment he shifted his position. It was only a slight movement, but she felt something—a button, a fingernail, *something*—scrape across the canvas against the taut, sensitive tip of her right breast.

One accidental movement, one rough touch, but it sent hot shards of pleasure streaking through her body, making her suck in a sharp gasp of shock.

"Is something wrong? Rae?"

"No . . . no, nothing's wrong."

But she was lying. Something was very wrong. She had been the biggest fool alive to think she could disregard her attraction to Tanner. It was too much to overlook, too big to ignore.

Even as she fought for control, he moved again. And again she felt the electric frisson of desire that caused her muscles to contract in automatic response. Her head tilted back, her spine arching involuntarily, and when she heard him speak again, when she heard the rasping whisper on the other side of the canvas, the words became lost somewhere in her dazed mind.

"What?" she said, breathless, confused. "I didn't hear you."

"Get closer." Temptation. Canvas-shrouded seduction. "Press a little closer, so you can hear over the water."

She should move away, she told herself. She should do it quickly, make it a definitive action. She should—

But already she was pressing her body more deeply into the cool, coarse cloth.

"Remember when I told you that your definition of lewd was different from mine?" His knuckles pressed through the canvas, moving, as though he were rubbing the muscles on his shoulder. "Do you find it lewd, the total freedom of those two people on the hill?" His signet ring scraped across her breasts, once, twice, three times, then slid lower, down her ribs to her stomach. "Does it embarrass you, the idea of sex without rules, without taboos, the thought of taking what you want without ever having to worry about whether or not it's quite civilized?"

The words weren't connecting with her brain. They were going straight to her body, urging her to get closer and even closer. And at that particular moment in time, his canvas-filtered touch on her aching body was more urgent, more important, than anything on earth.

Swallowing a whimper of pure need, Rae raised her eyes to the stars. She had to pull herself together. She had to break away before—

But even the thought of what might happen next was too much for her to handle. Dragging up more strength than she knew she possessed, she jerked away from the canvas panel.

And stepped directly under the water.

"What is it?" he asked when he heard her swear sharply under her breath. "What's happening?"

"I got my hair wet," she complained, her voice stiff.

He gave a low chuckle. "For a minute there I thought I had a convert, but look how fast you slipped back into civilization. Getting your hair wet isn't a disaster, sweetness. Let me tell you about making love in the rain."

"*No*. No, that's all right. The lesson was . . . effective," she said, already in the process of turning off the water, "but I think I'll just go in now and dry off."

It took fifteen minutes of leaning her head against the bathroom wall, her eyes tightly closed, her fists clenched into fists, before Rae finally felt her pulse return to normal.

He didn't know, she told herself. He couldn't know what he had done to her. He *couldn't*

It was only by telling herself over and over again that Tanner had no idea of what had taken place on her side of that canvas panel that Rae found the courage to put on the silk robe and leave the safety of the bathroom.

As they sat on the couch and talked, as Tanner forgot about the lesson and began the first normal conversation of their association, Rae tried desperately to take a step backward, back to the sane sensible person she had been before seeking Tanner's help, but it was no use. Something irreversible had taken place. She couldn't go back. It would be like asking a flower to become a seed again.

She would simply have to learn how to manage this new personality, she told herself, swallowing a sigh of relief when the buzzer on the dryer went off.

When she rose to her feet, Tanner stood as well, and there was a peculiar expression on his face, a glitter of something in his dark eyes, a smile that was almost rueful.

"What's that look for?" she asked, puzzled.

He gave a soft laugh and shook his head. "If you want to send Drew right out of his mind, you might consider wearing that tomorrow night."

Slowly lowering her head, she followed his gaze downward. The silk robe had slipped open, and the swells of her breasts were in plain view, only the tips covered.

Barely breathing, Rae didn't move when he reached out, took hold of the edges of the robe, and brought them together over her naked flesh, letting the backs of his thumbs scrape along the swells of her breasts. After smoothing down the lapels, he drew the belt tighter at her waist.

"There, now you're covered," he said, as though she were a child getting ready to go out into the snow. "Go on, scoot. You have to go home and rest up for tomorrow night."

Later, after she had dressed, after he had given her a few last-minute instructions and wished her good luck on her date with Drew, Rae opened her car door and took one last look back at the cabin.

The light was shining behind him, outlining his hard, lean body. And for one breathless moment, before she could push the thought away, she recalled an ancient sky, a grass-covered hill, and two naked, entwined bodies.

Turning into a flower was sometimes a very confusing process.

EIGHT

Tanner pulled into the parking lot of Rusty's Tavern, killed the motor, and leaned forward, resting his forearms on the steering wheel.

To the right, separated from Rusty's by a chest-high hedge, was the Dicton Café, a plain little name for a fancy little restaurant.

Rae and Drew were in there. Tanner had spotted Drew's white Lincoln parked on the other side, but even if he hadn't seen the car, he would have known they were there. It was where Drew always took his dates for coffee and dessert.

Tanner's lips twitched in a smile, and he wondered if Drew had gotten even a small glimpse of the woman Tanner had been with the night before. The real Rae. Intelligent and funny. Hiding her vulnerability behind a belligerent chin and a smart mouth. As sexy as hell but too naive to know it.

He almost laughed aloud when he thought of all the stupid advice he had given her. She didn't know that all she had to do was let down her guard a little and she would have every man in the Tri-county area baying at the moon. She didn't know—

There were a lot of things Rae didn't know.

After a moment he turned his head and stared at the blinking lights of the tavern. It had been more than six years since Tanner had gotten good and drunk. Tonight seemed as good a time as any to change that.

He climbed out of the truck and started toward the entrance. At the same moment the front door opened, and Marty Johnson walked out. Marty, a heavyset man with a perpetually sunburned face, was a local rancher with a small place about ten miles south of town. He was also Virg Embrey's brother-in-law.

Tonight, although Marty wasn't exactly dead drunk, he had gone pretty far over the line. He took several steps forward, then started stumbling to the side. When Tanner moved aside to let him pass, the rancher took a step in the same direction.

"Get outta my way," Marty muttered; then,

squinting his eyes and lowering his chin, he stared at Tanner. "Tanner. Tanner West. Don't you try and start something. Hear me?"

"You're drunk, Marty," Tanner said, his voice clipped. "I've got nothing against drunks. I plan on being one myself in a couple of hours, but I'm not going to stand here all night trying to guess which way you're going to move. You stand still, I'll walk around you."

When he took a step to the left, the other man moved with him, mumbling, "Virg shouldn'ta said what he did out at the country club."

Tanner knew by his tone that this wasn't in the way of a secondhand apology. Exhaling an impatient breath, he waited.

"I told 'im so," Marty continued. "I tol' him he had it dead wrong. Being Old Joe's bastard would be a step up for Tanner, I tol' Virg. Then at least half his blood wouldn't be from trash."

Shoving one hand in his back pocket, Tanner stared at the rancher. After a moment he said, "You smell like puke and look worse. Okay, now we've traded insults, what's next? Want to draw a line and dare me to step across it?"

Marty's features tightened. "You arrogant son of a bitch."

"No imagination," Tanner said, shaking his head in regret. "Look, if you want to fight, you don't have to beat around the bush. But before you start any-thing, you might want to think about what happened to Virg."

"You took him by surprise. In a fair fight he could take you . . . and so can I." He put a hand on Tanner's shoulder and pushed. "I don't think you're as tough as you make out." He pushed again. "Why don't we see?"

Tanner glanced up at the sky, then back at Marty. "You sure you want to do this? There's still time to back out with no harm done to your pride. Nobody would know except the two of us."

"You'd like that, wouldn't you?" The rancher pushed him again. "I hear Drew's out with that sweet little redheaded lawyer tonight. And I hear this one has Joe's blessing. What happens if they get married? What happens to you then, Tanner? What happens when Drew gives Joe a couple of grandkids? You'll be out in the cold, that's what. I don't think Drew'll mind making a few babies with that little gal. I bet he'll be on her so often—"

The words were cut off abruptly as Tanner grabbed Marty by the throat. The hot, restless spirit surged through his bloodstream, and all the demons inside him broke loose in a furious rush.

With a separate part of his mind, Tanner watched Marty draw back his fist. And in that instant he knew that the rancher had done him a good turn. This was just exactly what he needed tonight.

Rae was walking beside Drew along the little stone path that led through the Dicton Café's small Japanese garden when the commotion from next door reached them.

Stepping off the pathway, she moved closer, and even before she drew near the hedge she somehow knew what she would see.

In the parking lot of Rusty's Tavern, at the center of a small knot of people, Tanner had Marty Johnson by the collar, forcing him up against an old station wagon.

She caught her breath as Marty pulled free and hit Tanner in the mouth. Beside her, Drew gave a low chuckle and took her arm to lead her away from the hedge.

"Shouldn't someone make them stop?" she asked, glancing over her shoulder.

"Marty can take care of himself," Drew said, his voice unconcerned. "And even if he couldn't, Tanner always stops before he does much damage."

She wasn't worried about Marty. It was Tanner. Marty was shorter, but he was a good fifty pounds heavier.

"Why does he do it?" she wondered aloud.

"Tanner?" The man beside her shrugged. "Who knows? I think he enjoys it. For as long as I've known him, he's been fighting his way through life. That's just Tanner."

Drew had grown up with Tanner. He was used to his behavior and couldn't see what an outsider saw. Old Joe had probably been close to the truth when he said Tanner was fighting something inside himself.

Thirty minutes later Rae stood at her front door and watched Drew pull away from the curb. She couldn't even remember what they had talked about on the way home. Her mind, then as now, had been taken over with a problem named Tanner.

After locking the front door, she leaned against it for a moment, chewing absentmindedly at her bottom lip. He wasn't her problem. She knew that. And he wouldn't thank her for worrying about him. He thought he had life and his place in it all figured out. There was no way she could—

The thought died away when she realized that her distracted gaze had passed right over the man in her living room.

Tanner was sitting in an armchair, one long leg slung over the side as he flipped through her photo album.

Glancing up, he said, "Who's this?"

She put her purse on the hall table and walked

into the living room. Moving to stand beside him, she looked down at the picture he was pointing to.

"My uncle Titus. Great-uncle, actually. That old man always scared me to death. I don't know why. He was always yelling, 'You, girl, come here,' then laugh when I'd run and hide."

When he moved his finger to another picture, Rae sat on the arm of the chair, leaning down to look at the snapshot. "That's Aunt Boojie, my mother's adopted sister. She couldn't have children, so she compensated by spoiling me rotten. She was always bringing me little gifts, sneaking me chocolate-chip cookies when I got sent to my room."

He pulled something from the back of the album. "And this?" he asked with a grin.

She groaned aloud when she saw the picture of her as a young teenager. "I hate that picture. The shadows make my face look fat. I don't know why Mom sent it to me. She knows I hate it."

"Your face could never look fat. It's a good picture. You have a dreamy look in your eyes, like you're seeing things no one else can see. It's a good picture," he repeated.

"If you say—" She broke off and caught her breath, only now getting a close look at the cuts and bruises on his face.

"Look at you," she said, her voice both reproving

and concerned. "Come on, let me put something on those cuts."

Although she had expected him to object, he followed her to the bathroom and sat meekly on a white wicker stool while she cleaned the numerous cuts and abrasions.

"Don't keep me in suspense," he said when she had finished with a cut on his lip. "Spill your guts. Did you bring Drew to his knees?"

"Not quite."

"What—" He let out a loud yelp when she applied antiseptic to a cut on his cheek. "Holy hell, what is that stuff?"

"Stop whining. If you want to indulge in childish behavior, you have to pay the price."

Picking up his right hand, she shook her head over the scraped knuckles. She was glad she didn't have to see Marty Johnson's face. This fist had done some damage.

"Why are you so quiet?" he asked abruptly. "Are you still thinking about Prince Charming? Did he get you all hot and bothered tonight, Rae? Are you wondering how many dates you have to go on before you can ask him to come in?" His voice was harsh, his eyes cynically bored. "Drew would fit real well in that fluffy white bedroom of yours, but you'd better not let him have the goods too soon. Make him pant for a little while."

She glanced at him, one brow raised. "Just because you had a bad night is no reason to take it out on me."

Dropping his hand, she moved into the bedroom, barely aware that he followed her. How was she going to tell him? How was she supposed to break it to Tanner that all their work had been for nothing?

Drew was a good man. A nice, gentle man. But he wasn't the man for her. Tonight she had discovered an uncomfortable truth. She would never be able to feel anything more than friendship for Drew, and not even a close friendship. When he had kissed her at the front door, she had felt nothing. Nothing. All the sensuality Tanner had set loose in her had slept through the kiss.

She glanced over her shoulder and saw him standing near the window seat, watching her. There was no need to tell him anything, she decided. He would get Lynda just the way he had planned. Drew had lost interest in the blonde and wouldn't mind if Tanner started seeing her.

With a frown adding lines to her forehead, she sat on the bed. Drew wouldn't mind, but maybe Rae would. Tanner didn't need another strictly sexual relationship. He had had too many of those in the past.

Considering their history, it shouldn't have happened, but Tanner and she had become friends. Against all odds, and against the better judgment of both, they had gotten close. And now Rae wanted something more for him, something better than a lifetime of Lyndas. He needed a woman who would look beyond his sexy body, beyond the gleam of wildness in his eyes.

He needed the kind of woman who knew what forever meant.

Tanner was still watching her, his eyes dark and brooding as he waited for her to come out of her preoccupied silence.

Her lips curved in a rueful smile. "Have you ever thought how life has a way of making you wish you were a rock? Rocks are always either being worn down or built back up, but they don't care. Rocks just don't worry about it."

He drew back his head, one brow raised as he stared at her. "How whimsically philosophical."

She shook her head. "You look silly trying to raise your brow like that with your eye all swollen." She paused. "Why were you fighting?"

He shrugged his shoulders, then winced as the movement brought pain. "The guy was a butt-head and needed hitting."

"According to West's Law, they're all butt-heads. What was the real reason?"

He lowered himself to the window seat, moving

carefully. "He made a smart remark about my parents," he said without looking at her, "and I just happened to be in the mood to make him regret it."

"Your parents? I thought Old Joe—I mean . . ."

He gave a short laugh. "I know what you mean. You were there when Virg started spouting off about me being Joe's bastard. The stupid dipstick. If Virg had a brain, he'd know it couldn't be true. If I were Joe's son, you can bet he wouldn't keep it a secret. He'd go around telling everyone he knew, just to show he could get away with it."

"But Joe raised you?"

"No," he said, smiling, "I raised myself. Joe just gave me a place to do it."

She glanced down at her hands. "Glenna told me she remembers when you and your mother moved to town, but where was your father? Has it been a long time since you've seen him?"

"It will be twenty-eight years in October. I was seven last time I saw him. I have to say this for my old man, he may not have been perfect, but he damn sure knew how to make an exit."

There was genuine amusement in his laugh, but there was something that was not amusement in his eyes, something secret and painful.

"We were living in Abilene. Hadn't heard a word from him in six months, and then one day he just showed up."

He turned sideways and leaned against the side of the small alcove, a reminiscent smile curving his lips. "He took me out to eat. Italian food. I had spaghetti, he had pizza."

Catching her look, he shrugged one shoulder. "It's funny the things that stick in your memory. I guess it was because we didn't eat out very often. Anyway, when we got back to the house, the two of us sat out on the stoop for a long time, just listening to the night sounds. Dogs, police sirens, a radio somewhere down the street. After a while he started to talk. He told me he had made a lot of mistakes, but he was going to try and make it up to me. He was going to be a better father, the kind of father I deserved. He was going to take me fishing and buy me that red bicycle we saw at the discount store."

He drew in a slow breath and closed his eyes. "It was the most wonderful night of my life. I can still feel what I felt that night when I went to bed. I was so full of excitement and happiness, I could damn near see it in the room around me."

Opening his eyes, he met her look squarely. "When I got up the next morning, he was gone."

He paid no attention to her sharply indrawn breath, and when he continued, his voice was flat, empty of emotion. "He had taken everything of value in the house. It wasn't much, but it was all we had. I could have forgiven the stealing, I could have forgiven him for taking off without saying good-bye. But I never forgave the way he held out that little bit of hope, then pulled it out of reach again before I could grab hold."

Tilting his head back, he gave a short, rough laugh. "He said he was going to be the kind of father I deserved. For once in his life he was probably telling the truth. He probably thought he was giving me just exactly what I deserved."

Rae had to bite her lip to keep the tears back. Wrapping her arms tightly around her waist, she leaned forward, trying to contain the pain. Dear God, it hurt. It hurt as much as if it had happened to her. He had been seven years old. *Seven.* Too young, too vulnerable, to face that kind of disillusionment.

"What about your mother?" she asked in a hoarse whisper. "Where was your mother? Why didn't she stop him? Why didn't she—"

A short bark of laughter interrupted her. "You think I have a temper?" he said. "You should have seen her when she came home from one of her all-night romps and found out I let the old man steal the little bit of money she had stashed away."

He turned to raise the window, then glanced back at her. Whatever he had been about to say was lost as he took in the look on her face. He stared at her for a long moment before turning to lower one long leg out the window.

"I figured someone would have told you by now," he said, his voice curiously dead. "Everyone in town knows. My mother was a slut."

Before she could respond, before she could even take in what he said, he was out the window, sliding it shut behind him.

She walked to the window and as she stood, tears streaming down her face, and watched him vault over the back fence, the truth finally hit her.

She couldn't fall in love with Drew because she was already in love. With Tanner.

NINE

Once Rae had recognized the truth, she couldn't believe she hadn't seen it before. The way she had been fooling herself was almost funny. She had told herself that when she looked into his eyes and felt an instant bond, it was nothing but Lone Dees madness. She said that Tanner annoyed her. She said that he enraged her. She said that although he attracted her, it was only physical.

All lies. Rae hadn't wanted to accept what she was feeling, had denied it vehemently and often, because it scared her. The intensity scared her. The sheer magnitude of her feelings for him scared her.

As she sat at her desk the next day, she reached out and touched the portrait of Johnny, smiling as she ran her fingers over the dear features. What she was feeling now wasn't anything like what she had felt for her late husband. It wasn't warm and gentle. It wasn't comfortable and safe.

Loving Tanner was like that narrow mountain road he had told her about, full of hairpin turns and sheer drop-offs. But she had a feeling that if she ever made it to the top, the view would be spectacular and like nothing else on earth.

Getting there was the problem. Tanner never let anyone close to him. Last night she had wanted so badly to hold him, to rock him in her arms until some of the pain let go. But she knew by the rigid set of his jaw and the excluding look in his eyes that he wouldn't welcome comfort from her.

She leaned back in her chair and stared for a while at the ceiling. Tanner had told her about the wall society had built to keep itself separate from its own nature, but what he didn't say was that he, natural and wild as he was, had also built a wall. He had built a wall around his heart.

He didn't want Rae's love. He didn't need it. Tanner didn't need anyone. It hurt like hell to admit that to herself, but the sooner she learned to face facts, the better off she would be.

An instant later Rae sat up straighter. Better off? Without Tanner? What on earth was she thinking? She was sitting here in her dusty little office, and she was giving up. Without a fight, without a whimper.

She had become the old Rae again.

Rising to her feet, she stiffened her jaw. She wasn't that woman anymore. The new Rae fought for what she wanted.

"Hello, Tanner."

Rae had found him in the stables, forking fresh hay into one of the stalls. A dark horse tossed its head at Rae's approach, the dangerous gleam in its eyes matching that of his master.

"What are you doing here?" said Tanner. "We didn't set up another lesson."

"I'm not here for a lesson." She bit her lip, unsure of how to begin. Drawing in a deep breath, she said, "I wanted to talk to you about what you told me last night."

"What about it?" He made a short sound of contempt. "I can see your heart's bleeding all over the place. Do I look like I need pity?" He turned away from her, his back stiff. "I don't want to talk about it. And if I ever decide I do want to talk about it, I'll choose the time and place and confidant."

She nodded. "That's fair." The words were calm, but anger was slowly, surely, spreading through her. "But you see, I've gotten used to being your punching bag. I figure if you dump on me, it'll spare some poor innocent the grief."

"Leave it alone, Rae."

"Did you leave me alone?" She moved around to face him, her voice growing louder, more vehement. "In the two years I've been here, have you ever given me a break? You poke at me, you snipe at me, you pry into my thoughts and feelings. Why should I be more considerate than you've been?"

He reached out and grasped her arm, forcibly walking her toward the stable door. "Out," he rasped, the word stiff with control. "*Get out.*"

Jerking her arm free, she backed away from the door. "I won't. Not until you tell me the rest. Not until you tell me about your mother."

His dark eyes blazed with anger. "Rae, dammit—"

"I'm not moving," she said through tight lips.

Swinging around, he kicked the wall behind him with such force, a row of riding tackle fell clanging to the packed-earth floor. "You want to know about my mother? Fine, I'll tell you. I never disappoint a lady. And you are a lady. You couldn't in your wildest dreams imagine a woman like my mother. You think it was coming home and finding her in bed with a different man every night that bothered me? Hell, no. Kids adjust. They learn to accept."

He was pacing back and forth now, his features hard with anger. "But what I couldn't handle, what I never learned to accept, was leaving things behind."

He shot a glance at her. "You don't know what I'm talking about, do you? How could you? You lived in the same house all your life, you had your Johnny next door. You couldn't know what it was like coming home time after time to find her packing, knowing that we were going to leave everything behind again." He shook his head. "Sometimes it was the bill collectors, or maybe someone caught her dipping in the till at whatever joint she was working at. Sometimes she just got bored and decided to look for what she needed—whatever the hell that was—in the next town. Most of the time she didn't even give me enough warning to pack. Not that I had much. But what I had, I valued. And those poor miserable kids I claimed as friends, kids no one else would play with, I valued them too."

He gave a harsh laugh. "That changed. I learned better. I learned not to value anything, friends, possessions, nothing. Because sooner or later it got left behind."

She moved toward him, her heart twisting inside her chest. "Tanner—"

He held out a hand, backing away. "I'm not finished. I haven't got to the best part yet. We moved to Dicton when I was twelve. And this time something was different. We stayed. I didn't know why, but I didn't ask questions. She got herself a steady boyfriend, Tom Lyell, a man who was almost decent. He treated her right. Hell, he even treated me right."

Tilting his head back, he drew in an unsteady breath. "That kind of thing is a trap. You start hoping—"

He broke off and shook his head, as though trying to rid himself of the memory. "When we had been here almost six months, I started to hope that this time we would have a real home. Hope. Judas priest, how stupid can you get? You would think after what my father did, I would have learned better. But I was still young. That's the only excuse I have. I was too young to know what hope really is. Hope's just another way to lie to yourself, and don't let anybody tell you different."

He turned away from her, away from whatever he saw in her face. "In December, a week before Christmas vacation, school let out early, a gas leak in the lunchroom or something. I walked home the way I always did, and I was a block away when I spotted the strange car in the driveway. I don't know why, but as soon as I saw it, I started shaking. I was so scared, I couldn't catch my breath. I dropped my books and ran. When I got in the house, I didn't make a sound. As soon as I saw all the boxes in the hall, I went straight to her bedroom. I could hear them before I opened the door, and I knew what I'd find, but that didn't stop me."

His pause lasted only the span of two heartbeats, but Rae knew by the stiffness in his back that he was reliving the scene in his mind.

"As soon as she saw me in the doorway, she started screaming at me to get out. She was trying to cover herself with the sheet, and the guy with her was trying to get into his pants." He gave a short laugh. "I wasn't worried about seeing my mother without her clothes, and I wasn't worried that she was screwing some stranger. That didn't even bother me. I could only think of one thing. I stood there, with her swearing at me, the guy yelling at her, and I just kept asking over and over again, 'What about Tom?' "

He turned around and met her eyes, his lips twisting in a cynical smile. "I think my attitude may have pissed her off some. She jumped out of bed and grabbed me, holding her face right up against mine, calling me a twisted little bastard. Then she started to calm down. She was putting on her slip when she told me, in an offhand way, that we were leaving town with her new 'friend,' and if I wasn't ready in an hour, I'd get left behind."

He frowned. "I'm not sure what happened next. There's a blank space, then I remember standing in the driveway, and the man's car was minus a windshield. They said I threw a cement block through it. I don't remember.

"And that's the end of a pitiful little story," he said with a shrug. "She sent for the police, and I was shipped off to a center for juvenile delinquents." He gave a soft laugh. "I finally got to stay in one place."

He slowly turned his head and looked at her, taking in the tears running down her face. With two quick steps he had her by the shoulders, lifting her off her feet to give her a hard shake. "Don't look at me like that. Damn you—You wanted to know! You asked for this, so you can damn well take it."

He shook her again, snapping her neck. "Stop it! Don't cry for me. I don't need anybody to cry for me."

She wasn't listening to the words, she was looking at his eyes. Those dark, tormented eyes. Reaching up, she laid a trembling hand along the side of his face.

Drawing in a sharp breath, he closed his eyes, and when he opened them again, the demon light was blazing out of control.

"That was a mistake," he said, his voice ragged. "You set the devils loose, sweetness. Take my advice, and run while you've still got the chance."

Holding his gaze, she gave her head one short shake. She wouldn't run away from this part of him. She wanted it all. Everything he had in him. The anger and the pain. The raging wildness.

A groan caught in his throat, and he wrapped his arms around her, bringing her close as he covered her lips in a savage kiss.

"You don't know what you're doing," he whispered against her bruised lips a moment later. "It takes me over." Grasping her buttocks, he pulled her hard against him, telling her without words what was going to happen next. "I warned you to get out of the way. Now it's too late. *Too late.*"

His hands still on her buttocks, he lifted her, fitting her against his hard groin. With a breathless moan she wrapped her legs around his waist, pressing her lips to his as he moved toward the stall behind them.

"I'm going to do what I've been wanting to do since I first laid eyes on you," he whispered as he pressed her down to the hay and brought his hands to her aching breasts. "I want this," he told her. "And this." She felt his fevered touch on the inside of her thighs. "And this," he rasped out as he pushed an impatient hand beneath the waistband of the silk panties. "Sweet heaven, I want it all."

One finger was moving against the slick moisture between her thighs, sliding inside, and he gave a rough, triumphant laugh when her hips pushed against his hand in an involuntary movement.

Out of her mind with wanting him, she could only whisper, "Yes," over and over again, the word becoming frantic as she tore at his clothes, at her own. His devils were loose in her as well, making her writhe against his hard, naked body, making her cry out in desperate need.

"Let it go, Rae," he whispered, his voice hoarse with urgency as he moved his finger inside her. "Don't hold anything back. Let me inside. Let the wildfire take over, wrap it around me, and let it *burn me up*."

The next few minutes were a blur of surging, grasping intensity. He touched every inch of her, exploring all her secret places. He was inside her with his fingers, with his tongue, with his soul. He held nothing back and demanded the same of her.

No touch unthinkable, no act forbidden. Whatever felt good was right.

And when he entered her at last with one hard, urgent thrust, the world exploded in glorious, untamed pleasure, like nothing she had ever felt before.

As the shadows of evening began creeping into the stable, Tanner's strong, naked body lay close to hers. He leaned on one elbow, looking down at her as he ran a slow hand across her body. For a moment his fingers rested on the triangle of hair between her thighs.

"Ultima Thule," he whispered. "I can't get over this color."

Bending down, he kissed her there, then moved his head back and forth, letting the soft hair brush across his lips. When Rae caught her breath with stirring desire, he gave a soft laugh and raised his head to meet her eyes.

"You have hay in your hair," she said, her voice still husky.

"So do you. Miss Prim and Proper. Do you realize Loco was watching the whole time?"

When she shot a wary glance toward the horse, Tanner laughed again and rose to his feet, pulling her along with him.

"It's nature, remember? Loco doesn't care any more than the sky does."

She glanced around. "Where are my clothes?"

"I hid them. You don't need clothes out here. There's no one to see you . . . except me." He ran his gaze over her naked body. "And I definitely like what I see."

The look in his eyes made the tips of her breasts grow hard and brought a little throbbing pulse to her center. She glanced back at the hay.

"Uh-uh," he murmured, pulling her into his arms. "Hay might be natural, but any marks on this body"—he ran his hands over her hips—"I want to put there myself. We'll try the bed this time."

Rae pulled out of his arms and was halfway to the house before he caught up with her.

"What happened when you got out of the detention center?"

Hours had passed. They had tried the bed and the shower—the most incredible experience of her life—and even the armchair. Now they were back in his bed, side by side, her head resting on his shoulder.

Her question made him groan. "You don't let go, do you? I stayed in for a little over a year. That's where I learned to fight."

"Isn't that a long time for one windshield?"

"I guess, but my mother had left no forwarding address, and they couldn't just turn me loose. They ended up placing me in a foster home." He grinned. "I stayed there for almost two weeks, then I came back to Dicton. I was sleeping in a barn at Ashkelon when Joe found me. He fixed it with the authorities to let me stay, and I earned my keep working around the ranch."

He stared up at the ceiling. "He didn't have to do it. I was a stray that no one wanted. He didn't get anything out of it. But he let me stay."

"And that's why you continue to stay? That's why you don't go after your dream?"

He nodded. "As long as Joe needs me, I'll stay." After a moment he glanced down at her. "Are we through talking now?"

Before he finished the question, he ran a hand down her body and clasped her between the legs, tightening his fingers, then loosening them, then tightening them again.

Instantly Rae's heart began to pound with desire. Would she ever be able to get enough of him?

Raising her head, she sucked at his lower lip, then whispered, "We're through talking."

When Rae woke up, she was alone in the bed. Stretching her arms lazily, she glanced around the room. Her clothes were in a neat stack at the foot of the bed, and the smell of coffee was in the air.

Tanner stood at the window, his back to her, his forehead resting against the glass.

"Tanner?"

When he raised his head and turned it toward her, she knew instantly that something was wrong. The early morning light streaming through the window made his face look angular and hard.

"What is it?" she asked, sitting up. "What's wrong?"

"Wrong? There's nothing wrong." Even his voice had changed. The bored, cynical note was back. "In fact, I'd say you're coming along just fine. I never thought you'd make such a good student."

Her pulse was racing now as fear spread through her body. "I don't know what you're talking about."

"To tell you the truth," he said, as though she hadn't spoken, "I didn't expect the lessons to go this far. Not that I'm complaining. It's always good to get double duty out of something."

Wrapping her arms around her waist, she fought against the shivers that started the moment he turned to face her. "Double . . ."

"Teaching you how to be a woman so you can have a better shot at Drew and getting a little of the action myself," he explained, his voice impersonal.

She moistened her lips. "Are you trying to make me believe that what just happened was part of the *lessons*?"

Fierce anger surged through her bloodstream, then just as quickly it subsided. He was trying to make her mad. He was trying to make her hate him.

Studying his face, she said, "Why are you doing this?"

"Maybe a better question is, why did you?" He took a step toward her, lines of anger carved deep in his face. "Were you looking for a little walk on the wild side? Or maybe it was a pity hump? Well, I don't need it. I don't need you."

She was out of the bed now, standing in front of him, matching his fury with her own. "You think I did it because I felt *sorry* for you? Where were you? Which bed were you in? Not this one, that's for damn sure. There is no way anyone could interpret what happened in this bed as pity. It was magic, Tanner. It was *right*. I have never, not in my whole life, felt anything like—"

He broke in with a short sound of contempt. "Judas priest, there's nothing more dismal than rehashing sex. This"—he waved a hand at the bed—"was Lone Dees madness, two years overdue. If you weren't so freakin' civilized, and we could have gotten at each other that night, we would have. Well, now we've played it out. We did it. It was fun. Now it's over."

He shook his head and sent her a pitying look. "You think this was something special? God, how women love to delude themselves. I can get that kind of fun anywhere, any day of the week."

He stared at her for a moment, studying whatever he saw in her eyes, then he swung away, turning his back on her again.

"Lynda got back in town yesterday," he said, his voice flat. "I probably should have told you before, but then I wouldn't have been able to add the good lady lawyer to my list. Lynda is back, and she's receptive as hell. She wants me. No games, no hang-ups, just straightforward sex. I'm seeing her tonight . . . so there won't be any more lessons."

Somehow Rae got into her clothes and out the door. As she was stumbling down the steps, she heard him speak, and the words weren't much more than a rough whisper of sound.

"*See you, Rae.*"

TEN

Two days later Rae parked in front of her office and stepped from the car.

Sweet heaven, she was tired. She couldn't remember ever being so tired.

Tanner hadn't been in town in days, and Rae assumed he was off somewhere with Lynda. The thought didn't bring either anger or pain. She was simply numb. Everything had shut off. She did her work mechanically. And that's the way she ate and slept and moved. It was a state she recognized. Rae was grieving, the same way she had grieved when Johnny died.

Before she reached the door to her office, Glenna opened it and grabbed her arm. "There's a range fire out at Lyle Summer's place, and it's a doozy.

It's already wiped out a third of his spread, and it's getting into the trees now."

Turning around, Rae moved quickly back toward the car. "We'd better take your car," she threw over her shoulder. "I don't think mine will make it over the rough ground out there. Just give me fifteen minutes to change my clothes."

When something like this happened, it showed the best of small-town life. Everyone pitched in and worked together. Everyone cared.

Rae and Glenna, along with a dozen other women from town, spent the next two days making sandwiches and dishing up stew, serving coffee and iced tea to the men who were fighting the fire. They came back with black faces and dry throats that told of the fiery landscape they had left behind.

Only once in those two days did Rae catch a glimpse of Tanner, and the minute he caught her watching him, he turned his back on her and walked away.

On the third day, after the men had gained a measure of control over the fire, Rae was serving coffee to a group of men who sat on the tailgate of one of the dozens of pickups parked in the field.

After she had filled their cups, she moved around to the side of the truck, and as she stooped over to pull a grass burr from the leg of her jeans she heard them talking.

"I'll say one thing for him, no one here has worked harder to put out that fire."

Rae straightened but didn't move away. She knew without asking whom these men were talking about.

Another of the men made sounds of contempt. "He probably figures he needs to get used to the flames. He'll see enough of them in hell."

There was loud laughter, then the first man spoke again. "You're just sore because that little blonde out at the truck stop gets all flustered every time she sees him."

"You don't know nothing about nothing."

"I like him." This was a strong, quiet voice. "When that tornado took the roof off my barn, Tanner was there the next day, ready to help me get it all back together. He took my boy fishing a couple of times too."

"Well, saint or sinner, he's taking too many chances with that fire." The first man was speaking again. "He walks into it like he don't give a damn whether he comes out or not."

This wasn't the first time Rae had heard about Tanner's recklessness, and she was worried about him. Time after time, she watched the men come back to the field and others leave to take their places. But she hadn't seen Tanner in two days.

By late afternoon she couldn't stand it any

longer. Wondering what he was doing, wondering if he was being as careless as everyone said.

After talking to one of the men, she left the field behind and headed into the blackened landscape. The small copse where she found him was bare of undergrowth. It had all burned away. Everything had burned away. In every direction she looked, there was nothing but black ash and burned limbs.

Tanner, his face and hands covered in grime, sat on ground, leaning against a charred stump, his eyes closed.

"I brought you something to eat," she said without preamble.

He opened his eyes, and for one brief instant she saw in their dark depths that old restless hunger, so overpowering, it took her breath away.

She had already taken a step toward him before she remembered the last time she had gone to him. Stopping abruptly, she bit her lip.

He glanced at the sandwiches and thermos in her hands. "Another good deed?"

"That's right," she said, placing the food on the ground beside him.

Now that she knew he was all right, there was no reason for her to stay, she told herself. No reason at all.

But even as she was turning away, his voice stopped her.

"I saw you with Drew yesterday," he said abruptly. "You were looking after a burn on his hand. You two look like you're getting pretty tight. I guess the unholy alliance worked after all. Drew's perfect for you. The only one qualified to sit at Siege Perilous."

She glanced over her shoulder, one brow raised in inquiry. "Siege Perilous?"

"The seat reserved for the knight destined to bring back the Holy Grail," he explained, his voice dry. "No one else can sit there. It would be fatal if they tried."

She closed her eyes, then opened them again, swallowing hard. "You want me to be with Drew?"

A couple of seconds passed before he answered her, then the only thing he said was, "Drew's a good man."

A stiff gust of wind blew a strand of hair across her face. Brushing it aside, she stared at him, her chest tight with unhappiness. "Yes, Drew's a good man, but—"

A cracking noise, as loud as a thunderclap, sounded directly over her head. She heard Tanner call her name, and in the next instant he was diving at her, shoving her out of the way.

Rae rolled on the ground and almost immediately was on her feet again, looking around frantically for Tanner. The tree that had fallen covered most of the small copse, its charred limbs spreading across the blackened ground.

"Tanner!" she yelled, pulling at the branches, swearing viciously when they broke off under her fingers.

"What is it? What are you doing?"

Suddenly Drew was beside her, trying to pull her away from the tree.

"Glenna told me you were out here. What are you doing?"

She shook off his hands with an impatient jerk of her shoulders. "Tanner's under here," she said, her voice tight as she pulled at more of the branches. "Tanner's caught under—"

"I'm all right."

His voice came from the other side of the tree. Scrambling over the trunk and through the protruding limbs, she caught a glimpse of his shirt. "Tanner!"

"I'm all right," he repeated, his voice irritable. "It just knocked the wind out of me. If you'll move this thing a little to the right, I can squeeze out."

Together, she and Drew managed to break away most of the limb that was pinning Tanner to the ground, and several minutes later he rolled out from under the tree.

Rae knelt beside him, touching him, reassuring herself that he wasn't hurt.

With something that sounded like a groan of pain, Tanner pulled away from her and rose to his feet. "I told you I'm okay," he said tightly. "A couple of scratches and bruises. No big deal." Without looking at her, he pushed a rough hand through his hair and muttered, "Better get back to it."

And then he walked away, leaving her on her knees, staring after him.

It was only when she felt a hand on her shoulder that Rae remembered Drew. Rising to her feet, she glanced at him and winced at the look of sympathy in his eyes.

"You love him, don't you?" When she didn't answer, his lips twisted in a crooked smile. "You should have seen how white you were when you thought he was hurt. You looked like death." Frowning, he turned his head in the direction Tanner had gone. "You don't know him, Rae. I don't guess anyone really knows Tanner, but we've been friends for a long time, and he's told me enough for me to know his mother twisted something inside him." He met her eyes, concern etched into his gentle face. "I know it hurts, but you're better off this way. Tanner would take you to hell with him."

She pressed a hand to her mouth, holding back the short, choked laugh. "Do you really think that scares me?" she whispered. "With Tanner? I would go, Drew. Willingly and without a backward glance."

Tanner pulled his pickup out onto the highway and pressed his foot to the floor. The fire was well and truly out, but he didn't feel like hanging around, talking about it with the other men.

He didn't feel like much of anything. He couldn't stop thinking about Rae. He had been trying to stay out of her way, but that didn't stop the thoughts. The memories.

He wished he could really get something going with Lynda. Tanner had never been interested in the blonde, but he wished he could have made love to her, if only to wipe the night he had spent with Rae out of his memory. But he couldn't do it. Rae had a hold on him that was unbreakable.

He exhaled a slow, unsteady breath as he thought about the night they had spent together. He knew without a doubt that her Johnny had never been able to make her go wild like that. And Drew wouldn't be able to either. That part of her was only for Tanner.

It wasn't much, but at least it was something.

He never should have gotten involved with her. He knew it. He knew it from the beginning, but like an idiot, he went right ahead. He had wanted to punish her for the way she always looked at him, as though he didn't quite measure up. And he had wanted to see if he could shake her loose from her good-girl image. But the main reason Tanner had agreed to the lessons was that since the night he first saw her, he hadn't been able to get her out of his mind. And since that first night, he had wanted her.

And now he was paying for his stupidity.

Pulling over to the side of the road, he rested his forearms on the steering wheel and stared straight ahead. And as he stared, another memory came to him.

The year he had turned eight, the year after his father's last visit, Tanner had been invited to Lainie Browne's birthday party. It didn't matter that Lainie's mother had made her invite the whole class. Tanner had never been to a party before, and he didn't care why he had been invited.

He remembered ironing a white shirt, searching for a pair of jeans that didn't have a hole in the knees. And then he had walked to Lainie's house. It was all the way across town, but he didn't mind. He was going to a party.

It was only when he was inside her house, squeezed in with all the other kids, that he saw that everyone else was carrying a brightly wrapped package. They had all brought gifts. He felt stupid and crude for not knowing such a simple thing.

Tanner had brought nothing, and his hands felt awkward in their emptiness.

Moving slowly so as to draw no attention to himself, he backed quietly out of the room. The party wasn't for him. Tanner had nothing to offer.

Now, as he rested his chin on his hands, he gave a harsh laugh. It didn't take a psychologist to figure out why the memory came to him just now.

Although Drew was not good enough for Rae and never would be, he could at least give her what she was used to, what she deserved. Security. Peace of mind. Respectability. All wrapped up in bright, shiny paper.

The party wasn't for him. Because Tanner had nothing to offer.

A week after the fire, on her way back from lunch, Rae heard that Old Joe had died of a stroke. It was only two months ago that she had sat in his office with him, going over his will, and she wondered if he had had some kind of premonition. *There's a damned epidemic of it. People dropping like flies.*

Dicton wouldn't be the same without him. Drew would take over at Ashkelon, and although his would be a gentler reign, he would never have the personality of his father. Some of the wild flavor of Welch County was gone forever.

Joe had told her that he wasn't leaving Tanner much, and compared to Drew's inheritance it wasn't, but $200,000 was still a nice tidy sum. Enough—

Rae stopped in her tracks, feeling the blood drain from her face.

It was enough to allow him to follow his dream. Now that Joe was dead, Tanner was free to go.

She couldn't let it happen. Every night for a week, when she closed her eyes, she could see the look on his face that day she had found him sitting in the copse.

Tanner loved her. He might not want to love her, and he might be fighting against loving her. He might even be willing to make a mess of his life by denying his love for her, but Rae would be damned if she'd let him make a mess of hers as well.

Tanner didn't look up when she parked her Volvo behind the horse trailer that was hooked up to his green pickup. He didn't look up until she stood beside him and watched him load another box into the bed of the pickup.

"I heard about Joe," she said, her voice soft and hesitant. "I'm sorry, Tanner. I know you cared about him."

After a moment he leaned against the truck and looked out across the range. "Just before he died, he reached out and grabbed my arm, and he looked at me. He didn't say anything, he just looked at me. And that was when I knew. I knew he was saying good-bye to me as a father says good-bye to a son." He sucked in a slow breath. "I wouldn't ever take anything away from Drew, but I knew then that I'd had the best of Joe. Much more than Drew ever had. Even when we argued, we understood each other. We communicated in a way he and Drew never had."

After a moment he pushed away from the cab. "Well, guess I better get—"

Rae panicked. He was going to just walk away again. He was going to leave her behind, the way he had been forced to leave so many things behind in his life.

Catching hold of his arm she said, "Not yet. There are . . . there are things that need to be said. Things between us that are still unresolved." She moistened her lips in a nervous gesture. "Remember when you said there was a wildfire in me? I didn't believe you then. But gradually, bit by bit, I began to see it, I began to feel it. And then, when we made love, I knew that part of me was finally out in the open. It was really there. It had always been there. But you're the only one who ever saw it, Tanner. *The only one.* Doesn't that make you stop and think? Doesn't it make you wonder why it's only there for you?"

"You're talking about sex, Rae. Sex is just—"

"No," she broke in. "No, you're wrong. Sex is part of it, but it's a symptom, a side effect of something larger."

He shook his head. "You don't know what you're saying. Why do we have to rehash this—"

"Because you're telling lies!"

She drew in a trembling breath. She had to stay calm, she told herself, wiping damp palms on her jeans. She was fighting for her life. She had to find a way to make him understand, to make him really hear what she was saying.

"Johnny was—"

"I don't want to hear about Johnny," he said, the words sharp.

"Well, that's too bad. You're going to hear about him. You see, I used to think I wanted to love someone the way I loved Johnny, but I was wrong. That isn't what I want at all. I want more. Much more."

"So why are you telling me this?" He sounded angry. And desperate to get away from her. "If you want more than Johnny Good-as-gold, you'd better look up at the big house."

"Loving Johnny was so easy," she said, her voice soft with remembered love. "In fact, I almost made a conscious decision to love him." She raised her eyes to his. "With you, the decision was taken out of my hands. I couldn't *not* love you. My love for Johnny was a carefree first love. My love for you hits deeper, it makes me feel more than I ever thought possible."

She moved a step closer. "Johnny added something wonderful to my life. But you . . . Tanner, you *are* my life."

His blazing eyes moved restlessly across her face. "You don't know what you're saying," he said in ragged whisper.

"I do. I *do*." She tightened her lips to steady them. "I know what forever means, Tanner. That was one of the requirements, remember? A woman who knows what forever means. Well, I know. Forever is you."

When he simply stood there staring at her, helpless rage rose inside her, and she hit him in the chest with a tightly clenched fist. "*You bastard.* How many times do I have to come to you on my knees? How many times do I have to swallow my pride . . . and beg you . . . and beg you to . . ."

"*Don't.*" His face twisted as he reached out and pulled her into his arms. "Sweet heaven, Rae, don't cry like that. Don't, please. I'm sorry . . . I'm so sorry. I didn't—"

He broke off and framed her face with his hands. "You better mean this, Rae. No, listen to me. You better know what you're doing, because once I claim you, once I really make you mine, I won't ever be able to let you go. Not ever."

He was shaking all over, his fingers digging into her back. "I've spent every minute of the last few weeks telling myself not to fall for that hope-against-all-hope stuff again. Not this time, not when it was about you, not when it was more important than anything in my life."

"You stupid—" She broke off and shook her head. "Didn't you ever consider the possibility that I might feel the same way?"

His chin moved across the top of her head in short, rough strokes. "A couple of times I almost let myself wonder, but I stopped it before it got started." She couldn't see his face, but she could hear the ragged edges of leftover pain in his voice. "When I saw your car, I tried to tell myself you brought those out here because you're so damned nice. They were a gift to get me started on my dream."

He gave a choked laugh. "But I found out hope doesn't die that easy, not even in an outlaw."

Together they turned and looked at her car. Strapped to the top were two wooden rocking chairs.

Rae would be the woman, made special by his love, who sat beside him as they watched their children play.

THE EDITOR'S CORNER

July belongs to ONLY DADDY—and six magnificent heroes who discover romance, family style! Whether he's a confirmed bachelor or a single father, a small-town farmer or a big-city cop, each of these men can't resist the pitter-patter of little feet. And when he falls under the spell of that special woman's charms, he'll stop at nothing to claim her as a partner in parenting and passion. . . .

Leading the terrific line-up for July is Linda Cajio with **ME AND MRS. JONES**, LOVESWEPT #624. Actually, it should be *ex*-Mrs. Jones since high school sweethearts Kate Perry and Mitch Jones have been divorced for eleven years, after an elopement and a disastrous brief marriage. Now Kate is back in town, and Mitch, who's always been able to talk her into just about anything, persuades her to adopt a wise-eyed injured tomcat, with the promise that he'd be making plenty of house calls! Not sure she can play stepmother to his daughter Chelsea, Kate tells herself to run from the man who so easily ignites her desire, but she still remembers his hands on her body and can't send him away. To Mitch, no memory can ever match the heat of their passion, and he's been waiting all this time to reclaim the only woman he's ever truly loved. With fire in his touch, he sets about convincing her to let him in once more, and this time he intends to keep her in his arms for always. An utterly delightful story from beginning to end, told with Linda's delicious sense of humor and sensitive touch.

In **RAISING HARRY**, LOVESWEPT #625 by Victoria Leigh, Griff Ross is a single father coping with the usual problems of raising a high-spirited three-year-old son. He's never been jealous of Harry until he finds him in the arms of their neighbor Sharron Capwell. Her lush mouth makes Griff long to kiss her breathless, while her soft curves tempt him with visions of bare shoulders touched only by moonlight and his hands. She makes him burn with pleasure as no woman ever has, but Griff, still hurt by a betrayal he's never forgiven, insists he wants only a friend and a lover. Single and childless, Sharron has always been content with her life—until she thrills to the ecstasy Griff shows her, and now finds herself struggling with her need to be his wife and Harry's mother. Rest assured that a happily-ever-after awaits these two, as well as the young one, once they admit the love they can't deny. Victoria tells a compelling love story, one you won't be able to put down.

Who can resist **THE COURTING COWBOY**, LOVESWEPT #626 by Glenna McReynolds? Ty Garrett is a rough-edged rancher who wants a woman to share the seasons, to love under the Colorado skies. But he expects that finding a lady in his middle-of-nowhere town would be very rough—until a spirited visiting teacher fascinates his son and captivates him too! Victoria Willoughby has beautiful skin, a very kissable mouth, and a sensual innocence that beckons Ty to woo her with fierce, possessive passion. He awakens her to pleasures she's never imagined, teaches her how wonderful taking chances can be, and makes her feel alluring, wanton. But she's already let one man rule her life and she's vowed never to belong to anyone ever again. Still, she knows that finding Ty is a miracle; now if she'll only realize that he's the best man and the right man for her . . . Glenna's talent shines brightly in this terrific romance.

Bonnie Pega begins her deliciously sexy novel, **THEN COMES MARRIAGE**, LOVESWEPT #627, with the hero and heroine meeting in a very unlikely place. Single mother-to-be Libby Austin certainly thinks that seeing the hunk of her dreams in a childbirth class is truly rotten luck, but she breathes a sigh of relief when she discovers that Zac Webster is coaching his sister-in-law, not his wife! His potent masculinity can charm every stitch of clothing off a woman's body; too bad he makes it all too clear that a child doesn't fit into his life. Still, unable to resist the temptation of Libby's blue velvet eyes and delectable smile, Zac lays siege to her senses, and her response of torrential kisses and fevered caresses drive him even wilder with hunger. Libby has given him more than he's hoped for—and a tricky dilemma. Can a man who's sworn off marriage and vows he's awful with kids claim a wildfire bride and her baby? With this wonderful romance, her second LOVESWEPT, Bonnie proves that she's a name to watch for.

There's no sexier **MAN AROUND THE HOUSE** than the hero in Cindy Gerard's upcoming LOVESWEPT, #628. Matthew Spencer is a lean, muscled heartbreaker, and when he answers his new next-door neighbor's cries for help, he finds himself rescuing disaster-prone Katie

McDonald, who's an accident waiting to happen—and a sassy temptress who's sure to keep him up nights. Awakening his hunger with the speed of a summer storm, Katie senses his pain and longs to comfort him, but Matthew makes her feel too much, makes her want more than she can have. Though she lets herself dare to dream of being loved, Katie knows she's all wrong for a man who's walking a careful path to regain custody of his son. He needs nice and normal, not her kind of wild and reckless—no matter that they sizzle in each other's arms. But Matthew's not about to give up a woman who adores his child, listens to his favorite golden oldie rock station, and gives him kisses that knock his socks off and make the stars spin. The magic of Cindy's writing shines through in this enchanting tale of love.

Finishing the line-up in a big way is Marcia Evanick and **IN DADDY'S ARMS**, LOVESWEPT #629. Brave enough to fight back from wounds inflicted in the line of duty, Bain O'Neill is devastated when doctors tell him he'll never be a father. Having a family is the only dream that ever mattered to him, a fantasy he can't give up, not when he knows that somewhere there are two children who are partly his, the result of an anonymous sperm donation he made years ago. A little investigation helps him locate his daughters—and their mother, Erin Flynn, a fiery-haired angel who tastes as good as she looks. Widowed for two years, Erin takes his breath away and heals him with her loving touch. Bain hates keeping the truth from her, and though the children soon beg him to be their daddy, he doesn't dare confess his secret to Erin, not until he's silenced her doubts about his love and makes her believe he's with her to stay forever. All the stirring emotions and funny touches that you've come to expect from Marcia are in this fabulous story.

On sale this month from Bantam are three spectacular women's novels. Dianne Edouard and Sandra Ware have teamed up once again and written **SACRED LIES,** a spellbinding novel of sin, seduction, and betrayal. Romany Chase is the perfect spy: intelligent, beautiful, a woman who thrills to the hunt. But with her latest mission, Romany is out of her depth. Adrift in a world where redemption may arrive too late, she is torn between the enigmatic priest she has orders to seduce and the fierce agent she desires. Beneath the glittering Roman moon, a deadly conspiracy of greed, corruption, and shattering evil is closing in, and Romany must choose whom to believe—and whom to love.

With more than several million copies of her novels in print, Kay Hooper is indisputably one of the best loved and popular authors of romantic fiction—and now she has penned **THE WIZARD OF SEATTLE,** a fabulous, magical story of immortal love and mesmerizing fantasy. Serena Smyth travels cross-country to Seattle to find Richard Patrick Merlin, guided by an instinct born of her determination to become a master wizard like him. She knows he can be her teacher, but she never expects the fire he ignites in her body and soul. Their love forbidden by an ancient law, Serena and Merlin will take a desperate gamble and travel to the long-lost world of Atlantis—to change the history that threatens to keep them apart for eternity.

From bestselling author Susan Johnson comes **SILVER FLAME,** the steamy sequel about the Braddock-Black dynasty you read about in **BLAZE.** Pick up a copy and find out why *Romantic Times* gave the author its Best Sensual Historical Romance Award. Sizzling with electrifying sensuality, **SILVER FLAME** burns hot! When Empress

Jordan is forced to sell her most precious possession to the highest bidder in order to feed her brothers and sisters, Trey Braddock-Black knows he must have her, no matter what the cost. The half-Absarokee rogue has no intention of settling down with one woman, but once he's spent three weeks with the sweet enchantress, he knows he can never give her up. . . .

Also on sale this month, in the hardcover edition from Doubleday, is **THE PAINTED LADY,** the stunningly sensual debut novel by Lucia Grahame. All of Paris and London recognize Fleur not only as Frederick Brooks's wife, but also as the successful painter's most inspiring model. But few know the secrets behind his untimely death and the terrible betrayal that leaves Fleur with a heart of ice—and no choice but to accept Sir Anthony Camwell's stunning offer: a fortune to live on in return for five nights of unrestrained surrender to what he plans to teach her—the exquisite art of love.

Happy reading!

With warmest wishes,

Nita Taublib

Nita Taublib
Associate Publisher
LOVESWEPT and FANFARE

Don't miss these exciting
books by your favorite
Bantam authors
On Sale in May:

SACRED LIES
by Dianne Edouard
and Sandra Ware

THE WIZARD OF SEATTLE
by Kay Hooper

SILVER FLAME
by Susan Johnson

"SPECIAL SNEAK PREVIEW"
THE MAGNIFICENT ROGUE
by Iris Johansen
On Sale in August

SACRED LIES
by Dianne Edouard and Sandra Ware

On Sale in May

Romany Chase is the perfect spy: intelligent, beautiful, a woman who thrills to the hunt. But torn between the fierce Israeli agent she desires and the enigmatic priest she has orders to seduce, Romany is out of her depth—adrift in a world where redemption may arrive too late . . . .

As soon as Romany opened the door, she knew she wasn't alone. Someone waited for her. Somewhere in the apartment.

She had never carried a gun. There had never been a need. Even though Sully could have gotten her easy clearance, and had more than once urged her to take along some insurance. But her assignments never warranted it. Except that one time, in Geneva, and that situation had come totally out of left field.

She allowed her eyes to become adjusted to the gloom and, easing herself against the wall, moved to the edge of the living room. She searched the shadows. Strained to see something behind the thick lumps and bumps of furniture. Nothing. She crouched lower and inched closer to the door opening into her bedroom.

She peered around the corner. Whoever was in the apartment had switched on the ceiling fan and the small lamp that sat on a dressing table in the adjoining bath. The soft light cast the room in semidarkness, and she could make out the large solid shape of a man. He reclined easily upon her bed, a marshmallowy heap of pillows propped against his back. He hadn't bothered to draw back the covers, and he lay on top of the spread completely naked.

She should have run, gotten out of her apartment as quickly as possible. Except she recognized the hard muscles under the deeply tanned skin, the black curling hair, the famous smirk that passed for a smile. Recognized the man who was a cold-blooded killer—and her lover.

Romany moved through the doorway and smiled. "I'm not even going to ask how you got in here, David."

She heard his dark laugh. "Is that any way to greet an old friend?"

She walked farther into the room and stood by the side of the bed. She stared into the bright green eyes, still a surprise after all this time. But then everything about David ben Haar was a surprise. "Why don't you make yourself comfortable?"

"I am . . . almost." He reached for her hand and ran it slowly down his chest, stopping just short of the black hair at his groin.

She glanced down, focusing on her hand, pale and thin clasped inside his. She could hear her breath catch inside her throat. And as if that sound had been meant as some sort of signal, he pulled her down beside him.

She rested with her back against him, letting him work the muscles at her shoulders, brush his lips against her hair. She didn't turn when she finally decided to speak. "What are you doing here, David?"

"I came to see you." The words didn't sound like a complete lie.

She twisted herself round to look up at him. "That's terribly flattering, David, but it won't work."

She watched the smirk almost stretch into a real smile.

"Okay, I came to make sure that Sully is taking good care of my girl."

"I'm not your girl, David." She tried not to sound mean, or hurt, or anything. But she could feel the muscles of his stomach tighten against her back.

"You know Sully's a fucking asshole," he said finally. "What's he waiting on, those jerks to open up a concentration camp and gas a few thousand Jews?"

"David, Sully's not an asshole. . . . Hey, what in the hell do you mean?" She jerked around, waiting for an answer, watching his eyes turn cold.

"Gimme a break, Romany."

"Dammit, David, I don't have the slightest idea what you're talking about. Besides, what in the hell have concentration camps got to do with . . . ?" She stopped short, not willing to play her hand, even though David probably knew all the cards she was holding.

"Well, Romany, I can save you, and Sully, and all your little friends over at the CIA a whole helluva lotta trouble. Somebody—and I think you're deaf, dumb, and blind if you haven't pegged who that is—is stealing the Church blind, swiping paintings right off the museum walls, then slipping by some pretty goddamn good fakes."

She watched him stare at her from inside the darkness of her bed, waiting with that flirting smirk on his mouth for her to say something. But she didn't answer.

" . . . And the SOB at the other end of this operation"—he was finishing what he'd started—"whether your CIA geniuses want to admit it or not, is black-marketing the genuine articles, funneling the profits to a group of neo-Nazis who aren't going to settle for German reunification."

"Neo-Nazis?"

She could hear him grit his teeth. "Yeah, neo-Nazis. Getting East and West Germany together was just the first stage of their nasty little operation. They've got big plans, Romany. But they're the same old fuckers. Just a little slicker."

"David, I can't believe—"

"Shit, you people never want to believe—"

"Stop it, David."

He dropped his head and took in a deep staccatoed breath. She felt his hands move up her arms to her shoulders and force her body close to his. "Sorry, Romany." He sounded hoarse. Then suddenly she felt him laughing against her. "You know something"—he was drawing back—"you're on the wrong side, Romany. We wouldn't have these stupid fights if you'd come and work with me. With the Mossad."

"Yeah? Work with you, huh? And just what inducement can you offer, David ben Haar?" She pulled away from him and stood up.

Her feelings about David were a tangled mess—which, after she'd watched him board the plane for Tel Aviv thirteen months ago, she'd thought she could safely leave unwound. But here he was again, still looking at her with that quizzical twist to his lips that she couldn't help but read as a challenge.

She wanted his hands on her. That was the thought that kept repeating itself, blotting out everything else in her mind. Her own hands trembled as she pushed the hair away from her neck and began to undo the buttons at her back. Undressing for him slowly, the way he liked it.

She hadn't let herself know how much she'd missed this, until she was beneath the covers naked beside him, and his hands were really on her again, taking control, his mouth moving everywhere on her body. The pulse of the ceiling fan blended suddenly with the rush of blood in her ears, and David's heat was under her skin like fire.

She pressed herself closer against him, her need for him blocking out her doubts. She wanted his solidness, his back under her hands, the hardness of him along the length of her body. David ben Haar, the perfect sexual fantasy. But real. Flesh and blood with eyes green as the sea. She looked into his eyes as he pulled her beneath him. There was no lightness in them now, only the same intensity of passion as when he killed. He came into her hard, and she shut her eyes, matching her rhythm to his. To dream was all right, as long as you didn't let it go beyond the borders of your bed.

* * *

With one small edge of the curtain rolled back, David ben Haar could just see through the balcony railing where the red Alfa Romeo Spider was waiting to park in the street. Romany had been flying about the apartment when the car had first driven up, still cursing him for her half-damp hair, amusingly anxious to keep the priest from getting as far as her door.

"I could hide in the bedroom." He had said it from his comfortable position, lying still naked on her sofa. Laughing at her as she went past buttoning her dress, hobbling on one shoe back to the bedroom.

"I don't trust you, David ben Haar." She'd come back with her other shoe and was throwing a hairbrush into that satchel she called a purse.

"Romany?" He had concentrated on the intent face, the wild curls threatening to break loose from the scarf that bound them. "Morrow one of the bad guys?"

Picking up a sweater, she had looked over at him then, with something remarkably like guilt. "I don't know." She was going for the door. "That's what I'm supposed to find out."

Then she was gone, her heels rat-tatting down the stairs. High heels at Villa d'Este. Just like an American. They never took anything seriously, then covered it up with a cynicism they hadn't earned. Romany was the flip side of that, of course, all earnestness and innocence. She was smart and she had guts. But it wouldn't be enough to protect her. He got up.

As he watched now, the Spider was swinging into the parking space that had finally become available at the curb. The door opened and a man got out, turning to where Romany had just emerged from under the balcony overhang. The man didn't exactly match the car, he looked far too American. What he didn't look like was a priest.

He watched them greet each other. Very friendly. The compressor on the air conditioner picked that minute to kick in again, so he couldn't hope to hear what was said. The man opened the passenger door for her, then walked around to get in. They didn't pull out right away, and he was wondering why when he saw the canvas top go down. The engine roared up as they shot away from the curb. He could tell by the tilt of her head that Romany was laughing.

They had not spoken for some time now, standing among the tall cypress, looking out below to the valley. The dying sun had painted everything in a kind of saturated light, and he seemed almost surreal standing next to her, his fair aureole of hair and tall body in light-colored shirt and slacks glowing against the blackness of the trees.

They had played today, she and Julian Morrow. Like happy strangers who had met in Rome, with no history and no future. She had felt it immediately, the playfulness, implicit in the red car, in the way he wore the light, casual clothes. Like an emblem, like a costume at a party.

She had sat in the red car, letting the wind blow everything away from her mind, letting it rip David from her body. Forgetting the job. Forgetting that the man beside her was a priest and a suspect, and she a paid agent of the United States government.

They had played today. And she had liked this uncomplicated persona better than any he had so far let her see. Liked his ease and his sense of humor, and the pleasure he had seemed to find in their joyful sharing of this place. She had to stop playing now, but this was the Julian Morrow she must hold in her mind. Not the priest. Not the suspect in criminal forgery. But a Julian Morrow to whom she could want to make love.

He turned to her and smiled. For a moment the truth of her treachery rose to stick in her throat. But she forced it down. This was her job. She was committed.

She smiled back, moving closer, as if she might want a better view, or perhaps some little shelter from the wind. He must have thought the latter, because she felt his hands draping her sweater more firmly around her shoulders.

Time to take the advantage. And shifting backward, she pressed herself lightly against his chest, her eyes closed. She was barely breathing, feeling for any answering strain. But she could find no sense of any rejection in his posture.

She turned. He was looking down at her. His eyes, so close, were unreadable. She would never remember exactly what had happened next, but she knew when her arms went around him. And the small moment of her triumph when she felt him hard against her. Then she was pulling him down toward her, her fingers tangling in his hair, her mouth moving on his.

At the moment when she ceased thinking at all, he let her go, suddenly, with a gesture almost brutal that set her tumbling back. His hand reached for her wrist, didn't let her fall. But the grip was not kind or gentle.

His face was closed. Completely. Anger would have been better. She was glad when he turned away from her, walking back in the direction of the car. There would be no dinner tonight at the wonderful terraced restaurant he had talked about today. Of that she was perfectly sure. It was going to be a long drive back to Rome.

THE WIZARD OF SEATTLE
the unique new romantic fantasy from
Kay Hooper

On Sale in May

In the bestselling tradition of the time-travel romances of Diana Gabaldon and Constance O'Day-Flannery, Kay Hooper creates her own fabulous, magical story of timeless love and mesmerizing fantasy.

She looked like a ragged, storm-drenched urchin, but from the moment Serena Smyth appeared on his Seattle doorstep Richard Patrick Merlin recognized the spark behind her green eyes, the wild talent barely held in check. And he would help her learn to control her gift, despite a taboo so ancient that the reasons for its existence had been forgotten. But he never suspected that in his rebellion he would risk all he had and all he was to feel a love none of his kind had ever known.

Seattle, 1984

It was his home. She knew that, although where her certainty came from was a mystery to her. Like the inner tug that had drawn her across the country to find him, the knowledge seemed instinctive, beyond words or reason. She didn't even know his name. But she knew what he was. He was what she wanted to be, needed to be, what all her instincts insisted she had to be, and only he could teach her what she needed to learn.

Until this moment, she had never doubted that he would accept her as his pupil. At sixteen, she was passing through that stage of development experienced by humans, twice in their lifetimes, a stage marked by total self-absorption and the unshakable certainty that the entire universe revolves around oneself. It occurred in infancy and in adolescence, but rarely ever again, unless one were utterly unconscious of reality. Those traits had given her the confidence she had needed in order to cross the country alone with no more than a ragged backpack and a few dollars.

But they deserted her now, as she stood at the wrought iron gates and stared up at the secluded old Victorian house. The rain beat down on her, and lightning flashed in the stormy sky, illuminating the turrets and gables of the house; there were few lighted windows, and those were dim rather than welcoming.

It *looked* like the home of a wizard.

She almost ran, abruptly conscious of her aloneness. But then she squared her thin shoulders, shoved open the gate, and walked steadily to the front door. Ignoring the bell, she used the brass knocker to rap sharply. The knocker was fashioned in the shape of an owl, the creature that symbolized wisdom, a familiar of wizards throughout fiction.

She didn't know about fact.

Her hand was shaking, and she gave it a fierce frown as she rapped the knocker once more against the solid door. She barely had time to release the knocker before the door was pulled open.

Tall and physically powerful, his raven hair a little shaggy and his black eyes burning with an inner fire, he surveyed the dripping, ragged girl on his doorstep with lofty disdain for long moments during which all of her determination melted away to nothing. Then he caught her collar with one elegant hand, much as he might have grasped a stray cat, and yanked her into the well-lit entrance hall. He studied her with daunting sternness.

What he saw was an almost painfully thin girl who looked much younger than her sixteen years. Her threadbare clothing was soaked; her short, tangled hair was so wet that only a hint of its normal vibrant red color was apparent; and her small face—all angles and seemingly filled with huge eyes—was white and pinched. She was no more attractive than a stray mongrel pup.

"Well?"

The vast poise of sixteen years deserted the girl as he barked the one word in her ear. She gulped. "I—I want to be a wizard," she managed finally, defiantly.

"Why?"

She was soaked to the skin, tired, hungry, and possessed a temper that had more than once gotten her into trouble. Her green eyes snapping, she glared up into his handsome, expressionless face, and her voice lost all its timidity.

"I *will* be a wizard! If you won't teach me, I'll find someone who will. I can summon fire already—a little—and I can *feel* the power inside me. All I need is a teacher, and I'll be great one day—"

He lifted her clear off the floor and shook her briefly, effortlessly, inducing silence with no magic at all. "The first lesson an apprentice must learn," he told her calmly, "is to never—ever—shout at a Master."

Then he casually released her, conjured a bundle of clothing out of thin air, and handed it to her. Then he waved a hand negligently and sent her floating up the dark stairs toward a bathroom.

And so it began.

Seattle, Present

His fingers touched her breasts, stroking soft skin and teasing the hard pink nipples. The swollen weight filled his hands as he lifted and kneaded, and when she moaned and arched her back, he lowered his mouth to her. He stopped thinking.

He felt. He felt his own body, taut and pulsing with desire, the blood hot in his veins. He felt her body, soft and warm and willing. He felt her hand on him, stroking slowly, her touch hungry and assured. Her moans and sighs filled his ears, and the heat of her need rose until her flesh burned. The tension inside him coiled more tightly, making his body ache, until he couldn't stand to wait another moment. He sank his flesh into hers, feeling her legs close strongly about his hips. Expertly, lustfully, she met his thrusts, undulating beneath him, her female body the cradle all men returned to. The heat between them built until it was a fever raging out of control, until his body was gripped by the inescapable, inexorable drive for release and pounded frantically inside her. Then, at last, the heat and tension drained from him in a rush . . .

Serena sat bolt upright in bed, gasping. In shock, she stared across the darkened room for a moment, and then she hurriedly leaned over and turned on the lamp on the nightstand. Blinking in the light, she held her hands up and stared at them, reassuring herself that they were hers, still slender and pale and tipped with neat oval nails.

They were hers. She was here and unchanged. Awake. Aware. Herself again.

She could still feel the alien sensations, still see the powerful bronzed hands against paler, softer skin, and still feel sensations her body was incapable of experiencing simply because she was female, not male—

And then she realized.

"Dear God . . . Richard," she whispered.

She had been inside his mind, somehow, in his head just like before, and he had been with another woman. He had been having sex with another woman. Serena had felt what he felt, from the sensual enjoyment of soft female flesh under his touch to the ultimate draining pleasure of orgasm. *She had felt what he felt.*

She drew her knees up and hugged them, feeling tears burning her eyes and nausea churning in her stomach. Another woman. He had a woman somewhere, and she wasn't new because there had been a sense of familiarity in him, a certain knowledge. He knew this woman. Her skin was familiar, her taste, her desire. His body knew hers.

Even Master wizards, it seemed, had appetites just like other men.

Serena felt a wave of emotions so powerful she could endure them only in silent anguish. Her thoughts were tangled and fierce and raw. Not a monk, no, hardly a monk. In fact, it appeared he was quite a proficient lover, judging by the woman's response to him.

On her nightstand, the lamp's bulb burst with a violent sound, but she neither heard it nor noticed the return of darkness to the room.

So he was just a man after all, damn him, a man who got horny like other men and went to some woman who'd spread her legs for him. And often. His trips "out of town" were more frequent these last years. Oh, horny indeed . . .

Unnoticed by Serena, her television set flickered to life, madly scanned though all the channels, and then died with a sound as apologetic as a muffled cough.

Damn him. What'd he do, keep a mistress? Some pretty, pampered blonde—she had been blond, naturally—with empty hot eyes who wore slinky nightgowns and crotchless panties, and moaned like a bitch in heat? Was there only one? Or had he bedded a succession of women over the years, keeping his reputation here in Seattle all nice and tidy while he satisfied his appetites elsewhere?

Serena heard a little sound, and was dimly shocked to realize it came from her throat. It sounded like that of an animal in pain, some tortured creature hunkered down in the dark as it waited helplessly to find out if it would live or die. She didn't realize that she was rocking gently. She didn't see her alarm clock flash a series of red numbers before going dark, or notice that her stereo system was spitting out tape from a cassette.

Only when the overhead light suddenly exploded was Serena jarred from her misery. With a tremendous effort, she struggled to control herself.

"Concentrate," she whispered. "Concentrate. Find the switch." And, for the first time, perhaps spurred on by her urgent need to control what she felt, she did find it. Her wayward energies stopped swirling all around her and were instantly drawn into some part of her she'd never recognized before, where they were completely and safely contained, held there in waiting without constant effort from her.

Moving stiffly, feeling exhausted, Serena got out of bed and moved cautiously across the room to her closet, trying to avoid the shards of glass sprinkled over the rugs and the polished wood floor. There were extra lightbulbs on the closet shelf, and she took one to replace the one from her nightstand lamp. It was difficult to unscrew the burst bulb, but she managed; she didn't trust herself to flick all the shattered pieces out of existence with her powers, not when she'd come so close to losing control entirely.

When the lamp was burning again, she got a broom and dustpan and cleaned up all the bits of glass. A slow survey of the room revealed what else she had destroyed, and she shivered a little at the evidence of just how dangerous unfocused power could be.

Ironically, she couldn't repair what she had wrecked, not by using the powers that had destroyed. Because she didn't understand the technology of television or radio or even clocks, it simply wasn't possible for her to focus her powers to fix what was broken. It would be like the blind trying to put together by touch alone something they couldn't even recognize enough to define.

To create or control anything, it was first necessary to understand its very elements, its basic structure, and how it functioned. How many times had Merlin told her that? Twenty times? A hundred?

Serena sat down on her bed, still feeling drained. But not numb; that mercy wasn't granted to her. The switch she had found to contain her energies could do nothing to erase the memory of Richard with another woman.

It hurt. She couldn't believe how much it hurt. All these years she had convinced herself that she was the only woman in his life who mattered, and now she knew that wasn't true. He didn't belong only to her. He didn't belong to her at all. He really didn't see her as a woman—or, if he did, she obviously held absolutely no attraction for him.

The pain was worse, knowing that.

Dawn had lightened the windows by the time Serena tried to go back to sleep. But she couldn't. She lay beneath the covers staring up at the ceiling, feeling older than she had ever felt before. There was no limbo now, no sense of being suspended between woman and child; Serena knew she could never again be a child, not even to protect herself.

The question was—how was that going to alter her relationship with Merlin? Could she pretend there was nothing different? No. Could she even bear to look at him without crying out her pain and rage? Probably not. How would he react when she made her feelings plain, with disgust or pity? That was certainly possible. Would her raw emotion drive him even farther away from her? Or was he, even now, planning to banish her from his life completely?

Because he knew. He knew what she had discovered in the dark watches of the night.

Just before her own shock had wrenched her free of his mind, Serena had felt for a split-second *his* shock as he sensed and recognized her presence intruding on that intensely private act.

He knew. He knew she had been there.

It was another part of her pain, the discomfiting guilt and

shame of having been, however unintentionally, a voyeur. She had a memory now that she would never forget, but it was his, not hers. She'd stolen it from him . . . . And of all the things they both had to face when he came home, that one was likely to be the most difficult of all.

The only certainty Serena could find in any of it was the knowledge that nothing would ever be the same again.

SILVER FLAME
by Susan Johnson

On Sale in May

She was driven by love to break every rule.... Empress
Jordan had fled to the Montana wilderness to escape a cruel
injustice, only to find herself forced to desperate means to
feed her brothers and sisters. Once she agreed to sell her most
precious possession to the highest bidder, she feared she'd made
a terrible mistake—even as she found herself hoping it was the
tall, dark, chiseled stranger who had taken her dare and claimed
her ....

Empress stood before him, unabashed in her nudity, and
raising her emerald eyes the required height to meet his so
far above, she said "What *will* you do with me, Mr. Braddock-
Black?"

"Trey," he ordered, unconscious of his lightly command-
ing tone.

"What *will* you do with me, Trey?" she repeated correcting
herself as ordered. But there was more than a hint of impudence in her tone and in her tilted mouth and arched brow.

Responding to the impudence with some of his own, he
replied with a small smile, "Whatever you prefer, Empress,
darling." He towered over her, clothed and booted, as dark
as Lucifer, and she was intensely aware of his power and size,
as if his presence seemed to invade her. "You set the pace,
sweetheart," he said encouragingly, reaching out to slide the

pad of one finger slowly across her shoulder. "But take your time," he went on, recognizing his own excitement, running his warm palm up her neck and cupping the back of her head lightly. Trey's voice had dropped half an octave. "We've three weeks. . . ." And for the first time in his life he looked forward to three undiluted weeks of one woman's company. It was like scenting one's mate, primordial and reflexive, and while his intellect ignored the peremptory, inexplicable compulsion, his body and blood and dragooned sensory receptors willingly complied to the urgency.

Bending his head low, his lips touched hers lightly, brushing twice across them like silken warmth before he gently slid over her mouth with his tongue and sent a shocking trail of fire curling deep down inside her.

She drew back in an unconscious response, but he'd felt the heated flame, too, and from the startled look in his eyes she knew the spark had touched them both. Trey's breathing quickened, his hand tightened abruptly on the back of her head, pulling her closer with insistence, with authority, while his other hand slid down her back until it rested warmly at the base of her spine. And when his mouth covered hers a second time, intense suddenly, more demanding, she could feel him rising hard against her. She may have been an innocent in the ways of a man and a woman, but Empress knew how animals mated in nature, and for the first time she sensed a soft warmth stirring within herself.

It was at once strange and blissful, and for a brief detached moment she felt very grown, as if a riddle of the universe were suddenly revealed. One doesn't have to love a man to feel the fire, she thought. It was at odds with all her mother had told her. Inexplicably she experienced an overwhelming sense of discovery, as if she alone knew a fundamental principle of humanity. But then her transient musing was abruptly arrested, for under the light pressure of Trey's lips she found hers opening, and the velvety, heated caress of Trey's tongue slowly entered her mouth, exploring languidly, licking her sweetness, and the heady, brandy taste of him was like a fresh treasure to be savored. She tentatively responded like a lambkin to new, unsteady legs, and when her tongue brushed his and did her own unhurried tasting, she heard him groan low in his throat. Swaying gently against her, his hard length pressed more adamantly into her yielding softness. Fire raced downward to a tingling place deep inside her as Trey's strong, insistent arousal throbbed against the soft curve of her stomach. He held her captive with his large hand low on her back as they kissed, and she felt a leaping flame speed along untried nerve endings, creating delicious new sensations. There was strange pleasure in the feel of his soft wool shirt; a melting warmth seeped through her senses, and she swayed closer into the strong male body, as if she knew instinctively that he would rarefy the enchantment. A moment later, as her mouth opened pliantly beneath his, her hands came up of their own accord and, rich with promise, rested lightly on his shoulders.

Her artless naîveté was setting his blood dangerously afire. He gave her high marks for subtlety. First the tentative withdrawal, and now the ingenuous response, was more erotic than any flagrant vice of the most skilled lover. And yet it surely must be some kind of drama, effective like the scene downstairs, where she withheld more than she offered in the concealing men's clothes and made every man in the room want to undress her.

Whether artifice, pretext, sham, or entreating supplication, the soft, imploring body melting into his, the small appealing hands warm on his shoulders, made delay suddenly inconvenient. "I think, sweet Empress," he said, his breath warm on her mouth, "*next* time you can set the pace. . . ."

Bending quickly, he lifted her into his arms and carried her to the bed. Laying her down on the rose velvet coverlet, he stood briefly and looked at her. Wanton as a Circe nymph, she looked back at him, her glance direct into his heated gaze, and she saw the smoldering, iridescent desire in his eyes. She was golden pearl juxtaposed to blush velvet, and when she slowly lifted her arms to him, he, no longer in control of himself, not detached or casual or playful as he usually was making love, took a deep breath, swiftly moved the half step to the bed, and lowered his body over hers, reaching for the buttons on his trousers with trembling fingers. His boots crushed the fine velvet but he didn't notice; she whimpered slightly when his heavy gold belt buckle pressed into her silken skin, but he kissed her in apology, intent on burying himself in the devastating Miss Jordan's lushly carnal body. His wool-clad legs pushed her pale thighs apart, and all he could think of was the feel of her closing around him. He surged forward, and she cried out softly. Maddened with desire, he thrust forward again. This time he *heard* her cry. "Oh, Christ," he breathed, urgent need suffocating in his lungs, "you can't be a virgin." He never bothered with virgins. It had been years since he'd slept with one. Lord, he was hard.

"It doesn't matter," she replied quickly, tense beneath him.

"It doesn't matter," he repeated softly, blood drumming in his temples and in his fingertips and in the soles of his feet inside the custom-made boots, and most of all in his rigid erection, insistent like a battering ram a hair's breadth from where he wanted to be so badly, he could taste the blood in his mouth. It doesn't matter, his conscience repeated. She said it doesn't matter, so it doesn't matter, and he drove in again.

Her muffled cry exploded across his lips as his mouth lowered to kiss her.

"Oh, hell." He exhaled deeply, drawing back, and, poised on his elbows, looked down at her uncertainly, his long dark hair framing his face like black silk.

"I won't cry out again," she whispered, her voice more certain than the poignant depths of her shadowy eyes. "Please . . . I must have the money."

It was all too odd and too sudden and too out of character for him. Damn . . . plundering a virgin, making her cry in fear and pain. *Steady, you'll live if you don't have her*, he told himself, but quivering need played devil's advocate to that platitude. She was urging him on. His body was even more fiercely demanding he take her. "Hell and damnation," he muttered disgruntedly. The problem was terrible, demanding immediate answers, and he wasn't thinking too clearly, only feeling a delirious excitement quite detached from moral judgment. And adamant. "Bloody hell," he breathed, and in that moment, rational thought gained a fingertip control on the ragged edges of his lust. "Keep the money. I don't want to—" He said it quickly, before he'd change his mind, then paused and smiled. "Obviously that's not entirely true, but I don't ruin virgins," he said levelly.

Empress had not survived the death of her parents and the months following, struggling to stay alive in the wilderness, without discovering in herself immense strength. She summoned it now, shakily but determinedly. "It's not a moral dilemma. It's a business matter and my responsibility. I insist."

He laughed, his smile close and deliciously warm. "Here I'm refusing a woman insisting I take her virginity. I must be crazy."

"The world's crazy sometimes, I think," she replied softly, aware of the complex reasons prompting her conduct.

"Tonight, at least," he murmured, "it's more off track than usual." But even for a wild young man notorious as a womanizer, the offered innocence was too strangely bizarre. And maybe too businesslike for a man who found pleasure and delight in the act. It was not flattering to be a surrogate for a business matter. "Look," he said with an obvious effort, "thanks but no thanks. I'm not interested. But keep the money. I admire your courage." And rolling off her, he lay on his back and shouted, "*Flo!*"

"No!" Empress cried, and was on top of him before he drew his next breath, terrified he'd change his mind about the money, terrified he'd change his mind in the morning when his head was clear and he woke up in Flo's arms. Fifty thousand dollars was a huge sum of money to give away on a whim, or to lose to some misplaced moral scruple. She must convince him to stay with her, then at least she could earn the money. Or at least try.

Lying like silken enchantment on his lean, muscled body, she covered his face with kisses. Breathless, rushing kisses, a young girls's simple closemouthed kisses. Then, in a flush of boldness, driven by necessity, a tentative dancing lick of her small tongue slid down his straight nose, to his waiting mouth. When her tongue lightly caressed the arched curve of his upper lip, his hands came up and closed on her naked shoulders, and he drew the teasing tip into his mouth. He sucked on it gently, slowly, as if he envisioned a lifetime without interruptions, until the small, sun-kissed shoulders beneath his hands trembled in tiny quivers.

Strange, fluttering wing beats sped through her heating blood, and a curious languor caused Empress to twine her arms around Trey's strong neck. But her heart was beating hard like the Indian drums whose sound carried far up to their hidden valley in summer, for fear outweighed languor still. He mustn't go to Flo. Slipping her fingers through the black luster of his long hair, ruffled in loose waves on his neck, she brushed her mouth along his cheek. "Please," she whispered near his ear, visions of her hope to save her family dashed by his reluctance, "stay with me." It was a simple plea, simply put. It was perhaps her last chance. Her lips traced the perfect curve of his ears, and his hands tightened their grip in response. "Say it's all right. Say I can stay. . . ." She was murmuring rapidly in a flurry of words.

How should he answer the half-shy, quicksilver words? Why was she insisting? Why did the flattery of a woman wanting him matter?

Then she shifted a little so her leg slid between his, a sensual, instinctive movement, and the smooth velvet of his masculinity rose against her thigh. It was warm, it was hot, and like a child might explore a new sensation, she moved her leg lazily up its length.

Trey's mouth went dry, and he couldn't convince himself that refusal was important any longer. He groaned, thinking, there are some things in life without answers. His hand was trembling when he drew her mouth back to his.

A moment later, when Flo knocked and called out his name, Empress shouted, "Go away!" And when Flo repeated his name, Trey's voice carried clearly through the closed door. "I'll be down later."

He was rigid but tense and undecided, and Empress counted on the little she knew about masculine desire to accomplish what her logical explanation hadn't. Being French, she was well aware that *amour* could be heated and fraught with urgent emotion, but she was unsure exactly about the degree of urgency relative to desire.

But she knew what had happened moments before when she'd tasted his mouth and recalled how he'd responded to her yielding softness, so she practiced her limited expertise with a determined persistence. She must be sure she had the money. And if it would assure her family their future, her virginity was paltry stuff in the bargain.

"Now let's begin again," she whispered.

THE MAGNIFICENT ROGUE
by Iris Johansen

On Sale in August

From the glittering court of Queen Elizabeth to the barren island of Craighdu, THE MAGNIFICENT ROGUE is the spellbinding story of courageous love and unspeakable evil. The daring chieftain of a Scottish clan, Robert MacDarren knows no fear, and only the threat to a kinsman's life makes him bow to Queen Elizabeth's order that he wed Kathryn Ann Kentrye. He's aware of the dangerous secret in Kate's past, a secret that could destroy a great empire, but he doesn't expect the stirring of desire when he first lays eyes on the fragile beauty. Grateful to escape the tyranny of her guardian, Kate accepts the mesmerizing stranger as her husband. But even as they discover a passion greater than either has known, enemies are weaving their poisonous web around them, and soon Robert and Kate must risk their very lives to defy the ultimate treachery.

In the following scene, Robert and his cousin Gavin Gordon have come to Kate's home to claim her—and she flees.

She was being followed!

Sebastian?

Kate paused a moment on the trail and caught a glimpse of dark hair and the shimmer of the gold necklace about her pursuer's neck. Not Sebastian. Robert MacDarren.

The wild surge of disappointment she felt at the realization was completely unreasonable. He must have come at Sebastian's bidding, which meant her guardian had persuaded him to his way of thinking. Well, what had she expected? He was a stranger and Sebastian was a respected man of the cloth. There was no reason why he would be different from any of the others. How clever of Sebastian to send someone younger and stronger than himself to search her out, she thought bitterly.

She turned and began to run, her shoes sinking into the mud with every step. She glanced over her shoulder.

He was closer. He was not running, but his long legs covered the ground steadily, effortlessly, as his gaze studied the trail in front of him. He had evidently not seen her yet and was only following her tracks.

She was growing weaker. Her head felt peculiarly light and her breath was coming in painful gasps. She couldn't keep running.

And she couldn't surrender.

Which left only one solution to her dilemma. She sprinted several yards ahead and then darted into the underbrush at the side of the trail.

Hurry. She had to hurry. Her gaze frantically searched the underbrush. Ah, there was one.

She pounced on a heavy branch and then backtracked several yards and held it, waiting.

She must aim for the head. She had the strength for only one blow and it must drop him.

Her breath sounded heavily and terribly loud. She had to breathe more evenly or he would hear her.

He was almost upon her.

Her hands tightened on the branch.

He went past her, his expression intent as he studied the tracks.

She drew a deep breath, stepped out on the trail behind him, and swung the branch with all her strength.

He grunted in pain and then slowly crumpled to the ground.

She dropped the branch and ran past his body and darted down the trail again.

Something struck the back of her knees. She was falling!

She hit the ground so hard, the breath left her body. Blackness swirled around her.

When the darkness cleared, she realized she was on her back, her arms pinned on each side of her head. Robert MacDarren was astride her body.

She started to struggle.

"Lie still, dammit." His hands tightened cruelly on her arms. "I'm not—Ouch!"

She had turned her head and sunk her teeth into his wrist. She could taste the coppery flavor of blood in her mouth, but his grip didn't ease.

"Let me go!" How stupidly futile the words were when she knew he had no intention of releasing her.

She tried to butt her head against his chest, but she couldn't reach him.

"Really, Robert, can't you wait until the words are said for you to climb on top of her?" Gavin Gordon said from behind MacDarren.

"It's about time you got here," MacDarren said in a growl. "She's trying to kill me."

'Aye, for someone who couldn't lift her head, she's doing quite well. I saw her strike the blow." Gavin grinned. "But I was too far away to come to your rescue. Did she do any damage?"

"I'm going to have one hell of a headache."

Kate tried to knee him in the groin, but he quickly moved upward on her body.

"Your hand's bleeding," Gavin observed.

"She's taken a piece out of me. I can see why Landfield kept the ropes on her."

The ropes. Despair tore through her as she realized how completely Sebastian had won him to his way of thinking. The man would bind her and take her back to Sebastian. She couldn't fight against both MacDarren and Gordon and would use the last of her precious strength trying to do so. She would have to wait for a better opportunity to present itself. She stopped fighting and lay there staring defiantly at him.

"Very sensible," MacDarren said grimly. "I'm not in a very good temper at the moment. I don't think you want to make it worse."

"Get off me."

"And have you run away again?" MacDarren shook his head. "You've caused me enough trouble for one day. Give me your belt, Gavin."

Gavin took off his wide leather belt and handed it to MacDarren, who buckled the belt about her wrists and drew it tight.

"I'm not going back to the cottage," she said with the fierceness born of desperation. "I *can't* go back there."

He got off her and rose to his feet. "You'll go where I tell you to go, even if I have to drag—" He stopped in self-disgust as he realized what he had said. "Christ, I sound like that bastard." The anger suddenly left him as he looked at her lying there before him. "You're afraid of him?"

Fear was always with her when she thought of Sebastian, but she would not admit it. She sat up and repeated, "I can't go back."

He studied her for a moment. "All right, we won't go back. You'll never have to see him again."

She stared at him in disbelief.

He turned to Gavin. "We'll stay the night at that inn we passed at the edge of the village. Go back to the cottage and get her belongings and then saddle the horses. We'll meet you at the stable."

Gavin nodded and the next moment disappeared into the underbrush.

MacDarren glanced down at Kate. "I trust you don't object to that arrangement?"

She couldn't comprehend his words. "You're taking me away?"

"If you'd waited, instead of jumping out the window, I would have told you that two hours ago. That's why I came."

Then she thought she understood. "You're taking me to the lady?"

He shook his head. "It appears Her Majesty thinks it's time you wed."

Shock upon shock. "Wed?"

He said impatiently, "You say that as if you don't know what it means. You must have had instructions on the duties of wifehood."

"I know what it means." Slavery and suffocation and cruelty. From what she could judge from Sebastian and Martha's marriage, a wife's lot was little better than her own. True, he did not beat Martha, but the screams she heard from their bedroom while they mated had filled her with sick horror. But she had thought she would never have to worry about that kind of mistreatment. "I can never marry."

"Is that what the good vicar told you?" His lips tightened. "Well, it appears the queen disagrees."

Then it might come to pass. Even Sebastian obeyed the queen. The faintest hope began to spring within her. Even though marriage was only another form of slavery, perhaps the queen had chosen an easier master than Sebastian for her. "Who am I to marry?"

He smiled sardonically. "I have that honor."

Another shock and not a pleasant one. Easy was not a term anyone would use to describe this man. She blurted, "And you're not afraid?"

"Afraid of you? Not if I have someone to guard my back."

That wasn't what she meant, but of course he wouldn't be afraid. She doubted if he feared anything or anyone, and, besides, she wasn't what Sebastian said she was. He had said the words so often, she sometimes found herself believing him, and she was so tired now, she wasn't thinking clearly. The strength was seeping out of her with every passing second. "No, you shouldn't be afraid." She swayed. "Not Lilith . . ."

"More like a muddy gopher," he muttered as he reached out and steadied her. "We have to get to the stable. Can you walk, or shall I carry you?"

"I can walk." She dismissed the outlandish thought of marriage from her mind. She would ponder the implications of this change in her life later. There were more important matters to consider now. "But we have to get Caird."

"Caird? Who the devil is Caird?"

"My horse." She turned and started through the underbrush. "Before we go I have to fetch him. He's not far. . . ."

She could hear the brush shift and whisper as he followed her. "Your horse is in the forest?"

"I was hiding him from Sebastian. He was going to kill him. He wanted me to tell him where he was."

"And that was why he was dragging you?"

She ignored the question. "Sebastian said the forest beasts would devour him. He frightened me." She was staggering with exhaustion, but she couldn't give up now. "It's been such a while since I left him." She rounded a corner of a trail and breathed a sigh of relief as she caught sight of Caird calmly munching grass under the shelter of an oak tree. "No, he's fine."

"You think so?" MacDarren's skeptical gaze raked the piebald stallion from its swayback to its knobby knees. "I see nothing fine about him. How old is he?"

"Almost twenty." She reached the horse and tenderly began to stroke his muzzle. "But he's strong and very good-tempered."

"He won't do," MacDarren said flatly. "We'll have to get rid of him. He'd never get through the Highlands. We'll leave him with the innkeeper and I'll buy you another horse."

"I *won't* get rid of him," she said fiercely. "I can't just leave him. How would I know if they'd take good care of him? He goes with us."

"And I say he stays."

The words were spoken with such absolute resolution that they sent a jolt of terror through her. They reminded her of Sebastian's edicts, from which there was no appeal. She moistened her lips. "Then I'll have to stay too."

MacDarren's gaze narrowed on her face. "And what if Landfield catches you again?"

She shrugged and leaned her cheek wearily against Caird's muzzle. "He belongs to me," she said simply.

She could feel his gaze on her back and sensed his exasperation. "Oh, for God's sake!" He picked up her saddle from the ground by the tree and threw it on Caird's back. He began to buckle the cinches. "All right, we'll take him."

Joy soared through her. "Truly?"

"I said it, didn't I?" He picked her up and tossed her into the saddle. "We'll use him as a pack horse and I'll get you another mount to ride. Satisfied?"

Satisfied! She smiled brilliantly. "Oh yes. You won't regret it. But you needn't spend your money on another horse. Caird is really very strong. I'm sure he'll be able to—"

"I'm already regretting it." His tone was distinctly edgy as he began to lead the horse through the forest. "Even carrying a light load, I doubt if he'll get through the Highlands."

It was the second time he had mentioned these forbidding Highlands, but she didn't care where they were going as long as they were taking Caird. "But you'll do it? You won't change your mind?"

For an instant his expression softened as he saw the eagerness in her face. "I won't change my mind."

Gavin was already mounted and waiting when they arrived at the stable a short time later. A grin lit his face as he glanced from Kate to the horse and then back again. "Hers?"

Robert nodded. "And the cause of all this turmoil."

"A fitting pair," Gavin murmured. "She has a chance of cleaning up decently, but the horse . . ." He shook his head. "No hope for it, Robert."

"My thought exactly. But we're keeping him anyway."

Gavin's brows lifted. "Oh, are we? Interesting . . ."

Robert swung into the saddle. "Any trouble with the vicar and his wife?"

Kate's hands tensed on the reins.

"Mistress Landfield appeared to be overjoyed to give me the girl's belongings." He nodded at a small bundle tied to the saddle. "And the vicar just glowered at me."

"Perhaps he's given up."

"He won't give up," Kate whispered. "He never gives up."

"Then perhaps we'd better go before we encounter him again," Robert said as he kicked his horse into a trot. "Keep an eye on her, Gavin. She's almost reeling in that saddle."

Sebastian was waiting for them a short distance from the cottage. He stood blocking the middle of the path.

"Get out of the way," Robert said coldly. "I'm not in the mood for this."

"It's your last chance," Sebastian said. "Give her back to me before it's too late."

"Stand aside, Landfield."

"Kathryn." Sebastian turned to her and his voice was pleading. "Do not go. You know you can never wed. You know what will happen."

Robert rode forward and his horse's shoulder forced Sebastian to the side of the trail. He motioned Gavin and Kate to ride ahead. "It's over. She's no longer your responsibility." His voice lowered to soft deadliness. "And if you ever approach her again, I'll make sure I never see you repeat the mistake."

"You'll see me." Landfield's eyes shimmered with tears as his gaze clung to Kate. "I wanted to spare you, Kathryn. I wanted to save you, but God has willed otherwise. You know what has to be done now."

He turned and walked heavily back toward the cottage.

"What did he mean?" Gavin asked as his curious gaze followed Landfield.

She didn't answer as she watched Sebastian stalk away. She realized she was shivering with a sense of impending doom. How foolish. This was what he wanted her to feel, his way of chaining her to him.

"Well?" Robert asked.

"Nothing. He just wanted to make me afraid." She moistened her lips. "He likes me to be afraid of him."

She could see he didn't believe her and thought he would pursue it. Instead he said quietly, "You don't have to fear him any longer. He no longer holds any power over you." He held her gaze with a mesmerizing power. "I'm the only one who does now."

OFFICIAL RULES TO WINNERS CLASSIC SWEEPSTAKES

No Purchase necessary. To enter the sweepstakes follow instructions found elsewhere in this offer. You can also enter the sweepstakes by hand printing your name, address, city, state and zip code on a 3" x 5" piece of paper and mailing it to: Winners Classic Sweepstakes, P.O. Box 785, Gibbstown, NJ 08027. Mail each entry separately. Sweepstakes begins 12/1/91. Entries must be received by 6/1/93. Some presentations of this sweepstakes may feature a deadline for the Early Bird prize. If the offer you receive does, then to be eligible for the Early Bird prize your entry must be received according to the Early Bird date specified. Not responsible for lost, late, damaged, misdirected, illegible or postage due mail. Mechanically reproduced entries are not eligible. All entries become property of the sponsor and will not be returned.

Prize Selection/Validations: Winners will be selected in random drawings on or about 7/30/93, by VENTURA ASSOCIATES, INC., an independent judging organization whose decisions are final. Odds of winning are determined by total number of entries received. Circulation of this sweepstakes is estimated not to exceed 200 million. Entrants need not be present to win. All prizes are guaranteed to be awarded and delivered to winners. Winners will be notified by mail and may be required to complete an affidavit of eligibility and release of liability which must be returned within 14 days of date of notification or alternate winners will be selected. Any guest of a trip winner will also be required to execute a release of liability. Any prize notification letter or any prize returned to a participating sponsor, Bantam Doubleday Dell Publishing Group, Inc., its participating divisions or subsidiaries, or VENTURA ASSOCIATES, INC. as undeliverable will be awarded to an alternate winner. Prizes are not transferable. No multiple prize winners except as may be necessary due to unavailability, in which case a prize of equal or greater value will be awarded. Prizes will be awarded approximately 90 days after the drawing. All taxes, automobile license and registration fees, if applicable, are the sole responsibility of the winners. Entry constitutes permission (except where prohibited) to use winners' names and likenesses for publicity purposes without further or other compensation.

Participation: This sweepstakes is open to residents of the United States and Canada, except for the province of Quebec. This sweepstakes is sponsored by Bantam Doubleday Dell Publishing Group, Inc. (BDD), 666 Fifth Avenue, New York, NY 10103. Versions of this sweepstakes with different graphics will be offered in conjunction with various solicitations or promotions by different subsidiaries and divisions of BDD. Employees and their families of BDD, its division, subsidiaries, advertising agencies, and VENTURA ASSOCIATES, INC., are not eligible.

Canadian residents, in order to win, must first correctly answer a time limited arithmetical skill testing question. Void in Quebec and wherever prohibited or restricted by law. Subject to all federal, state, local and provincial laws and regulations.

Prizes: The following values for prizes are determined by the manufacturers' suggested retail prices or by what these items are currently known to be selling for at the time this offer was published. Approximate retail values include handling and delivery of prizes. Estimated maximum retail value of prizes: 1 Grand Prize ($27,500 if merchandise or $25,000 Cash); 1 First Prize ($3,000); 5 Second Prizes ($400 each); 35 Third Prizes ($100 each); 1,000 Fourth Prizes ($9.00 each) ; 1 Early Bird Prize ($5,000); Total approximate maximum retail value is $50,000. Winners will have the option of selecting any prize offered at level won. Automobile winner must have a valid driver's license at the time the car is awarded. Trips are subject to space and departure availability. Certain black-out dates may apply. Travel must be completed within one year from the time the prize is awarded. Minors must be accompanied by an adult. Prizes won by minors will be awarded in the name of parent or legal guardian.

For a list of Major Prize Winners (available after 7/30/93): send a self-addressed, stamped envelope entirely separate from your entry to: Winners Classic Sweepstakes Winners, P.O. Box 825, Gibbstown, NJ 08027. Requests must be received by 6/1/93. DO NOT SEND ANY OTHER CORRESPONDENCE TO THIS P.O. BOX.

Don't miss these fabulous Bantam women's fiction titles on sale in June

LADY VALIANT

☐ 29575-6 $5.50/6.50 in Canada
by Suzanne Robinson
Bestselling author of LADY DEFIANT

"An author with star quality....Spectacularly talented."
—*Romantic Times*

Once Mary, Queen of Scots, had been her closest friend. Now Thea Hunt was determined to pay back the queen's kindness—by journeying to Scotland to warn her away from a treacherous marriage. But in the thick of an English forest, Thea suddenly finds herself set upon by thieves...and chased down by a golden-haired highwayman who'd still her struggles—and stir her heart—with one penetrating glance from his fiery blue eyes.

MASK OF NIGHT

☐ 29062-2 $4.99/5.99/6.50 in Canada
by Lois Wolfe
Author of THE SCHEMERS

"Fast paced, highly evocative, filled with action, surprises, and shocking revelations....an intriguing, different Civil War romance." —*Romantic Times* on *The Schemers*

In St. Louis in the late 1800s, a fair-haired beauty and a bankrupt cattleman hell-bent on revenge are drawn to each other across the footlights...but the heat of their passion would ignite a fire that could burn them both.

Ask for these books at your local bookstore or use this page to order.

☐ Please send me the books I have checked above. I am enclosing $ _____ (add $2.50 to cover postage and handling). Send check or money order, no cash or C. O. D.'s please.

Name _____

Address _____

City/ State/ Zip _____

Send order to: Bantam Books, Dept. FN105, 2451 S. Wolf Rd., Des Plaines, IL 60018
Allow four to six weeks for delivery.
Prices and availability subject to change without notice.   FN105 6/93

The Very Best In Contemporary Women's Fiction

Sandra Brown

_____	29085-1	22 INDIGO PLACE .... $4.50/5.50 in Canada
_____	56045-X	TEMPERATURES RISING $5.99/6.99
_____	28990-X	TEXAS! CHASE $5.99/6.99
_____	28951-9	TEXAS! LUCKY $5.99/6.99
_____	29500-4	TEXAS! SAGE $5.99/6.99
_____	29783-X	A WHOLE NEW LIGHT $5.99/6.99

Tami Hoag

_____	29534-9	LUCKY'S LADY $4.99/ 5.99
_____	29053-3	MAGIC $4.99/ 5.99
_____	29272-2	STILL WATERS $4.99/ 5.99
_____	56050-6	SARAH'S SIN $4.50/ 5.50

Nora Roberts

_____	27283-7	BRAZEN VIRTUE $4.99/5.99
_____	29597-7	CARNAL INNOCENCE $5.50/6.50
_____	29490-3	DIVINE EVIL $5.99/6.99
_____	29078-9	GENUINE LIES $4.99/5.99
_____	26461-3	HOT ICE $4.99/5.99
_____	28578-5	PUBLIC SECRETS $4.95/5.95
_____	26574-1	SACRED SINS $5.50/6.50
_____	27859-2	SWEET REVENGE $5.50/6.50

Pamela Simpson

_____	29424-5	FORTUNE'S CHILD $5.99/6.99

Deborah Smith

_____	29690-6	BLUE WILLOW $5.50/ 6.50
_____	29092-4	FOLLOW THE SUN $4.99/ 5.99
_____	29107-6	MIRACLE $4.50/ 5.50